WHY THE DEVIL CHOSE

NEW ENGLAND FOR HIS WORK

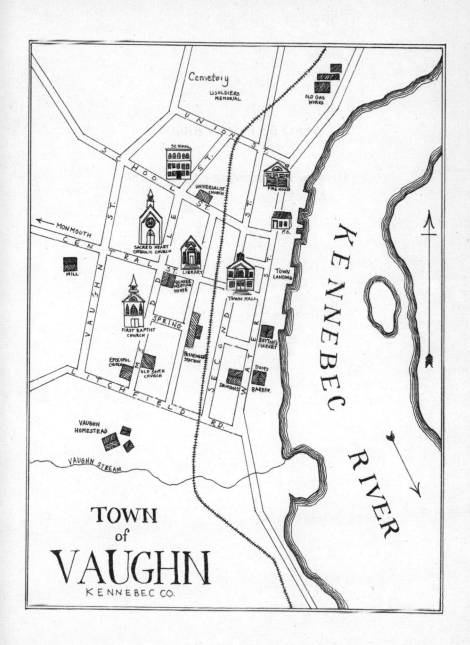

Cemetery

U.SOLDIERS MEMORIAL

OLD GAS WORKS

UNION ST.

SCHOOL ST.

SCHOOL

UNIVERSALIST CHURCH

FIRE HOUSE

MONMOUTH

CENTRAL

SACRED HEART CATHOLIC CHURCH

P.O.

MILL

ST.

UNION ST.

LIBRARY

QUAKER MEETING HOUSE

TOWN LANDING

TOWN HALL

VAUGHN ST.

DOE ST.

SPRING

FIRST BAPTIST CHURCH

PASSENGER STATION

BOTTANS MARKET

SECOND ST.

WATER ST.

EPISCOPAL CHURCH

OLD SOUTH CHURCH

DAWSONS

DOWS

BARBER

LITCHFIELD RD.

VAUGHN HOMESTEAD

VAUGHN STREAM

KENNEBEC RIVER

TOWN
of
VAUGHN
KENNEBEC CO.

ALSO BY JASON BROWN

Driving the Heart and Other Stories

WHY THE DEVIL CHOSE
NEW ENGLAND FOR HIS WORK

Stories by

JASON BROWN

 OPEN CITY BOOKS

New York

Printed in the United States of America

These stories were originally published in the following publications: "She" in *Harper's*; "Trees" in *Fish Stories*; "The Lake" and "Life During Peacetime" in *TriQuarterly*; "Why the Devil Chose New England for His Work" in *Epoch*; "Dark Room" in *StoryQuarterly*; "River Runner" in *Portland Magazine*; "North" in *Open City*; and "Afternoon of the *Sassanoa*" in *The Atlantic*.

Map by Kirstin Valdez Quade

Library of Congress Control Number: 2007935190
ISBN-10: 1-890447-47-1
ISBN-13: 978-1-890447-47-2

OPEN CITY BOOKS
270 Lafayette Street
New York, NY 10012
www.opencity.org

08 09 10 11 12   10 9 8 7 6 5 4 3 2

Open City Books are published by Open City, Inc., a nonprofit corporation.

For K. V. Q.

TABLE OF CONTENTS

SHE

Everything Natalie said seemed, to herself, to have been said better by him. He was less fond of speaking, however, than he was of hitting people in the face, which seemed a more likely source of her love to those of us who were in speech class with him. It could be, we reasoned, she was in love with the kind of things he might say if he spoke more often.

It was easy for someone like David Dion to be casual about fate. He was still in junior high, but high school girls picked him up in their daddies' cars and had sex with him out at the pit. No one I spoke to on a regular basis had even been to the pit. He was not anyone's boyfriend, didn't need to be. It was hard to guess how old he was if you didn't already know, if he hadn't tumbled down into your grade from the grade above when he was held back. He couldn't be that smart, you could tell, from the way he grinned at himself, but he was smart enough to know he didn't have to be loyal to any one girl.

Dion fought high school boys all the time; that was nothing; once he broke his fist against the face of a man in his twenties before getting his own nose smashed against the pavement. In school he sat two seats away from me in homeroom, where he spilled over his desk, stroking his thin mustache and cracking his knuckles, one handed, one finger at a time. In wood shop we were partners, making a gun rack. I made the rack, he kept it. He slouched back in his chair, his elbows on the sill, looking out the window from the corner of his eye like a prisoner. Not even the shop teacher said anything. They were related, kids said. He was related all over, mostly in the next county, where every other ice fisherman was an uncle, every other woman behind the cash register an aunt, and the rest cousins. He could walk into any store out there and borrow ten bucks; he owed everyone, even me, at least that much. I lent him one dollar at a time. He rolled the bills into joints and smoked them or sold them for two dollars, making a few bucks, he said, for later at the bar.

When Mr. Dawson of Dawson's Variety was told by one of his basketball players that Dion, their center, was in love with Natalie, he pictured the ridge of her muscle extending up from her knee into her track shorts. He had seen her the day before with Ron, the high school boy she went with, who was going to drop out to start in the air-conditioning business with his father so he and Natalie could get married as soon as possible. Her best friend, Denise, whose information was no better than second hand at this point, said, Well, it wasn't Love with Ron. Mr. Dawson overheard this. Denise was standing in his store with her friends Kristy and Francis waiting to buy a diet soda.

"I thought," Mr. Dawson said from behind the counter, "she was with that boy Ron."

"Well, she was," Denise said, secretly pleased at being the center of attention. "It just wasn't love," she said, her voice rising. "Anything but. Just a thing. This is Love."

My friend Andy's mother said, shaking her head while sitting at their kitchen table with a half dozen of her friends, that Natalie had bloomed too early. That's why people thought she should stay with Ron, who was a good thing in the long run, even though he was homely, with a protruding jaw and blemishes over his cheeks, and he was older. He was one of the Catholic boys, who would wait, and by the time they were ready and married she would have lost her looks, be heavy and distended, those legs thick as posts; just when no one else wanted her he would be there with enough desire stored up to blind his true sight for a lifetime.

One of the things Natalie loved about Dion was that he always let the other guy have the first shot. He never in his life coldcocked a guy. He let them know first, sometimes days in advance. Someone would tell the guy, and they would meet. If the guy went down, the fight was over. That was one of the things she loved about him. Dion walked away, or sometimes helped the guy to his feet. Once you get over the fear of getting hit, the same every time, he told me in wood shop, it doesn't matter what happens.

When Natalie's mother first heard that her daughter was in love with Dion, she said nothing, only stared at the wall. She was one of the last to know; people were afraid to tell her at first. Finally Mrs. Dawson called up to tell her while pretending she must already know. "You mean you don't know? Oh, my." Maybe, Mrs. Dawson was thinking, Natalie's mother will do something now.

Most of Natalie's clothes came directly from her mother's sewing machine, but they were not cheap looking on her. Every article was made to fit every precocious curve. Her father, on disability from the Bath Iron Works, was rarely seen except at the Wharf having a few or driving around in his truck scratching his beard with his CAT hat low over his brow. He could only see out of one eye.

Before Dion, she and Ron would walk down the hill after school, passing my house, crossing the tracks, on their way to the public library, which was where a lot of us went, strange to say, when we had nothing else to do. They walked alone, holding hands, had been going out since she was in sixth grade, he in junior high. In sixth grade people kissed on the playground, Missy D. and Kevin R. yelling at each other across the lunch room, the curses from their lips exactly the opposite of the intoxicated delight and fear on their faces, and there was even a story of David M., the short calm kid, getting a hand job at the movie theater. But no one went out, went steady, held hands in public at that age, except them. Ms. Hegel, the librarian, had no worries when they sat down to hold hands across the top of the reading table. Others had to be watched and checked on, would be up to nasty business in the stacks among the geography books. Ron and Natalie would only kiss each other for half a minute on the grass in front of the library while waiting for his mother to pick him up for dinner, and then her mother would come pick her up. Later they would talk on the phone for thirty minutes, no longer, according to his mother's rules. His mother worried that her mother made no rules. A girl should have rules, his mother said.

Occasionally people saw them kissing in front of the library. Mr. Wally drove by and happened to stop at the corner and look in their direction. Mr. Dawson, on his way to practice, saw them once. Her father saw them once, other kids saw them. I saw them, as I stepped out of the library door. They did not realize I was there. They sat on the steps two feet apart and strained their necks sideways to have their lips meet for this one moment, no more, before he checked to see if his mother was rounding the corner yet. Her mother was often late, and once did not arrive at all. Mr.

Dawson, returning from practice, just before dusk, saw her sitting there, knees pulled up, and offered her a ride home.

My mother must have forgotten, she said, with her hands clamped between her knees, palms out. But Mr. Dawson suspected it was more than that—everyone suspected, and he asked her if everything, honestly, everything, was all right. Everyone knew everything was not what it should be in that vinyl-sided house at the edge of a field her grandfather had once owned but father had sold off one piece at a time. Mr. Dawson, Ron's former coach, said she could talk candidly, that she could trust him, but not even Ron had ever been inside her house. When asked this time by Mr. Dawson, she responded in the same way she always did: Everything is fine. I'm just tired is all.

At first it was hard to believe she and Dion were together at all. No one saw them holding hands or even talking in the daylight. Denise reported seeing them kissing in the dark behind the school, and she was the first to confront Natalie about it, about Ron. Ron's over, she said. How? Denise wanted to know. How did this happen? Natalie shrugged her shoulders.

When she and Dion first got together, she insisted: Not in the daylight, not on Central Street by Dawson's or Tom's Pizza, not in his brother's car, which he drove only at night because he didn't have a license, even if his father's brother was a cop and didn't care. People saw them, though, at the fringe of the bonfire's light out at the pit or down by the river at the landing on one of the benches out of reach of the fluorescent lights.

At the same time Mr. Dawson heard that she was in love with Dion, he heard that Dion had quit his basketball team. He went into the back room after Denise and her friends left and leaned his forehead into his hand. They are in love, Denise had said. Nothing from her mouth had ever interested him before this statement. He tried not to think of Natalie. She ran track; she had been into the store with her mother, with Ron. Ron with acne. When he closed his eyes he saw her tanned thigh last summer as she sat on the bench outside the store, her blue shorts scrunched up above a pale line, the knob of her shoulder beneath her yellow sweater, and the curve at the corner of her mouth, which would harden into a battered smirk, he knew, by the time she was his age—by the time she was half his age.

That afternoon the basketball team stood on the court in their practice gear, not bouncing the ball, staring off in different directions, in disbelief that Dion had quit for her. Mr. Dawson was late; he was never late. They couldn't believe Dion was with her right now. Maybe off in his brother's car or at his cousin's house, where both parents worked, or off in Vaughn woods by the pond, or out by the pit waiting for it to get dark, or down by the river near the landing waiting for it to get dark. Any of them would have traded places with Dion. The game of basketball suddenly seemed pointless next to the thought of his hand on her hip, and she in her green slacks and yellow sweater burying her face in his flannel shirt, curling her fingers into his back, closing her eyes to hide, even from herself, how much she loved him.

When Mr. Dawson arrived, the team was sitting on their practice balls and on the bench, with their heads low. They hadn't noticed him come in, fingers splayed out in the air. The game of basketball seemed to him a cruel drama written to parody his frustration, and now he was forced to be its director.

They had only been together for a day, but it seemed to Natalie as if they had been together forever. There seemed no need to tell him anything; with one glance she knew he knew the years they had not been together were little more than preparation for this moment. She could tell from the turn of his hand hanging out the window of his brother's car what he was thinking about. He was thinking about her. When he looked at her she had to look away. When he thought about her, she was thinking about him. When he looked away, she looked at him; when she looked away, she could feel him looking at her. She realized now that she had always been looking for him, even though they had been in school together, sitting just a few seats away, standing across the playground from each other, he with his friends at the corner of the school parking lot by the Dumpster, she with hers by the swing sets. She had seen him but not seen him. She had been alive but not alive, until now.

On the second day she was not in school in the yellow linen shorts her mother had sewn together from Mrs. Nason's old drapes. There were only a few places she could be.

Two days later there was a teacher's meeting after school to discuss the situation, about which no one, least of all the principal, a tall man with Baptist visions, had anything to say. What can we do? Mr. Wally pleaded, his voice gruffer than usual. This was not, in other words, a passing thing. They could not just hold their breaths. The basketball team would not get to the championship, and every day, the men knew, glancing quickly at each other, they would have to see her leaving at the end of the day, as the days got warmer toward June, in her pink flannel shorts, or the blue satin ones, and the white silk shirt or the tank tops, the red bands holding her hair back from her cheeks, walking down the hill, not with Ron, but to be with *him* in all the dark crannies of the town, wrapped in nothing but his old jacket, arcing her pale stomach toward the moon, her open mouth barely giving voice to her thought: Dion.

"What about your mother?" Dion asked as they were walking by the river. "She comes to pick you up outside the library."

She was surprised he knew this, that he had been paying attention to her long before today. Maybe she was right about the way love worked; it had been planned all along.

"My mother can wait," she said and pulled him forward, down toward the trees. She leaned into him with her hands flat against his chest. He couldn't breathe. Her lips tasted a little of spaghetti sauce. He pulled her closer and she let her body stand flat against his for a moment before pushing away. He reached for her pants, but she pushed his hand back, explaining to him that love has its natural course. She took both his hands in hers and stood very close to him without touching him. She explained that if they rushed love it would shatter like glass.

"Like glass," he repeated, amazed at the way she put it. She was like no one he had ever met. He closed his eyes as she touched his face, covered his lips with her fingers. When he opened his eyes again, she was running back up the trail.

"I'll see you tomorrow," she yelled and was gone.

The rotting smell of the riverbank came to him, and he noticed for the first time that the sky was cloudy and the air quickly growing cool. But everything seemed different, somehow luminescent, awash with mercurial light. He sat down on a rock and watched the water swirl in the current.

In the following days she formed a list of things she wanted to have and do and be, without Ron. A boat, but not any boat, a giant motor sailer they could take all the way down the coast to Florida, so big there could be a storm and they wouldn't even notice down in their cabin below, where there would be a fireplace and a television-VCR in one. Who would be sailing the boat? Dion wanted to know. They would hire someone for that. But the rest of their life was imagined in modest proportions: dogs, golden collie mixes, not pure at all; three children; a house where everyone had a bedroom and there was one extra for a guest; and some land with a view of the hills around town. She didn't want to live down by the river or so close to a neighbor that you could see in their window at night. She had never thought of living anywhere else? He had thought of Montana. Montana—the word sounded chewed in her mouth. God, she said, shaking her head. Other places. Gardner? Farmingdale? Monmouth? Those places, the only other places she knew, were bad enough. Imagine what people were like even further away. No, she wanted to go to Florida, though. Not to live, just to go there as the Nasons did every winter, taking their daughter Julie with them so that she came back with a tan, even if she did look like a squirrel. And no matter what time of year it was Natalie would have fresh flowers in every room of the house. This idea from her mother, of how people really lived. And a horse in a red barn for her daughter. And light blue carpeting in every room. Our room, she said, with a canopy bed, but he didn't know what one was. It has a kind of roof, like a tent, she explained. He didn't see the point but pictured it anyway, a bed with a tent in a room that already had a ceiling and above that a roof. He had pictured a cabin in Montana where you could look up and see the nails from the roof shingles coming through. And lavender, she said. No one would be allowed to smoke. Every room would smell of lavender. Like me, she said, and pressed her wrist to his nose. This was the smell of their future.

None of us had been in love, not really, until now. Anything we had called love came back to us as mockery in the face of this sudden flight from reason. Andy had said he was in love with Missy, and it was a shame Missy was not in love with him. A daily lament rose from him like the steam of the heat from the pipes at school. Andy's mother hit the counter with her fist. "They're too young," she said, talking about Natalie and Dion, and we knew she was talking about their tongues running along the inside of each other's teeth and the suddenly anxious too-tight grip of her hand between his legs, and the taste of each other's skin, and the smell of each other's bodies, and the feel of him slipping inside her and her settling down over him, the shape of her mouth, the shape of his. She was talking about their bodies but thinking about the words they had used. Everyone knew. "Love," she finally growled, as if the creature itself had risen from her dreams to take over her kitchen. She gripped a package of spaghetti as if it was a club and stared at the wall, paralyzed by the idea of them out there.

They hadn't been going out for a week when she got in his brother's car and rode out to the next county. They ate at a Howard Johnson's. She ordered an ice cream sundae and he ordered a grilled cheese sandwich to go, in case she wanted to go all of a sudden. She ate her sundae and ordered a milk shake; he couldn't eat. He bought her a blue shirt in a fancy store, a boutique. It's a nice shirt, he said. It looks nice on you. It's a blouse, she said, turning for him in the parking lot with her eyes closed. A blouse, he repeated.

She made him drive faster, clinging to his arm, with her lips pecking gently against the nape of his neck. God, she said, God. Her breath smelled of chocolate. His eyes watered when she rested her hand on his knee and started to rub his thigh as if he were cold. She rubbed until his leg burned. Her stomach rose and sank over the gentle slopes as Dion pressed down harder on the pedal. The road to Monmouth was straight and rolling, the Firebird rising and falling as if with the swells of a heavy sea, the shocks rattling in a drum roll. Slow down, she said, but he didn't. What's in Monmouth? she wanted to know but didn't want to know. There was no reason to know, even though she had heard and did know. The bar everyone had heard about, the Chanticleer, that no one, at least no one from Bigelow Junior High, had been to. We heard it smelled of a cellar after a flood, the sweet twinge of wet walls and soaked carpets on a warm day.

It was a low windowless building tucked under a maple tree between the side of the road and a trickling stream, no light outside except the one BUD sign. This beer, golden from the tap, was sweeter than what Ron had given her, stolen from his father's icebox. She sat in the back of the room, far away from the others at the pool table, and stared down into her glass. She took a sip and put the mug down. He came over from the pool table and traced his finger along her lower lip, leaned over to kiss her. He loved her in that yellow sweater, her breasts weighted, pushing against the soft fabric, her yellow hair, each strand distinct, falling around her chin. She didn't want him to put on any music, she didn't want to play pool, she didn't want to have another beer, she didn't want to sit alone so many miles from home, she didn't want to be sitting under the bar light, dissected in its brightness at the end of this numberless dark road. So he took the keys to the car, the hell with the rest, and they drove all the way up to Monmouth over the Kennebec River and back again.

They held hands all the way; he said nothing and she loved the way he said it. She didn't want to go home, and so they kept going in another direction. All the roads looked the same at night. She said it clearly to him, LOVE, just before dawn, and he was afraid as they parked by a river, further away from home than she had ever been, of touching her. So she touched him as she had seen herself touch him in her mind, and just as she had imagined he held absolutely still. If he said anything, he said what she thought he would say, he said what she wanted him to say, what we all wanted to hear, things he had never said to anyone before, words he had never thought before, whose meaning he would not have been able to explain but felt as he said them as clearly as he felt her breath on his neck, as surely sweet as her hair was soft, as clearly as he felt he was not the same and would not ever want anything, anyone, as much as he wanted her.

The night she didn't come home, the first night ever, people thought of her bruised and bleeding in the corner of some motel room halfway between Vaughn and Mississippi. Others thought of her in the Hyatt in Boston, or they wouldn't wait so long: the Marriott in Portsmouth. Or they were on a cruise, on the *Scotia Prince* headed for Halifax, gambling in black tie and satin dress. And still others said, shaking their heads, No, no, she was gone, long gone from us, lying somewhere by the railway tracks. The man in the caboose will find her the next time we hear the Boston and Maine. She's somewhere between Haymarket and Bangor, bleeding into the gravel, her linens smudged, silk torn, the blush of her cheeks chalk white, and Dion halfway to Mexico. Andy was the only one who got it right, the more obvious answer: they lay side by side in the back of his brother's car parked on the edge of a field in the next county. She pulled the blanket beneath her chin as he pulled her head against his chest and ran a single finger through her hair. When she tilted her head, only her bangs and her lips caught the moonlight.

Everywhere Andy and I went was in search of her, just as Mr. Dawson drove up and down Litchfield Road and all the way across town to the quarry and back saying to himself he was on an errand when he was really hoping, just for a moment, to catch a glimpse of her. Her father was out looking for her now, too, in the truck, rifle at his side. Two of her uncles were on opposite sides of the town, covering all the roads leading in and out. Her mother told herself she had known the time would come; but not like this, she said to herself. Not with him. She had thought of Ron and the wedding, the white dress she would sew (had already spent hours, days, years, shaping it in her mind). Even if they found her, she would not be the same now.

The members of the basketball team, sure now that they would lose the final game of the season and miss the playoffs, were home with their parents watching television or eating potato chips or talking on the phone or listening to their parents talking in the next room or lying on their backs thinking of Dion out there with her; they listened to the sound of crickets and cars passing and shouts from up the street and dogs barking and pots clinking in the sink and footsteps of sisters on stairways while they thought of him out there touching her neck with the tips of his fingers before looking away to drive the car or order another beer or wave to his brother, as if the practicalities of living could distract him, even for a second, from where he would touch her next.

"He took her, he took her," Natalie's mother moaned over and over to her husband and his brothers.

"He dragged her off. He threw her in his car and took her away." Natalie's father was on the phone, calling Sheriff Chuck Sheldon and everyone he knew, which was everyone, the fathers of all the basketball players, fathers of daughters who were Natalie's friends, younger brothers of fathers of Natalie's friends and basketball players, fathers of girls not yet old enough to be in junior high, though when they were another Dion would be waiting for them.

All over town parents of girls who would be like or wanted to be like her and boys who might think of doing what he had done lay in bed staring at the ceiling, saying a few words to each other: What do you think? We'll find them tomorrow. What will you do? Don't know. Do you think she's all right? I really don't know. They didn't mention what they were thinking to their children, listening to them talk from the next room, giving voice to their thoughts of what might be happening out there, what he might be doing to her. No image, no story, once started, would complete itself in their minds: she was tied in the backseat, the purple, no the pink silk shirt, ripped down the front and her pale breasts shivering in the moonlight with her nipples like cherries on cream pie—where was he? Hovering above her. Just a hand comes into view; he was gentle now that he had what he wanted. Or she was running down the road in front of his headlights. They had pulled off the road, and she had gotten away, though just for a moment. Her blouse had been stripped off and was lying torn somewhere out of view, probably in the backseat or on the side of the road, and she ran just in her white panties with the cloth riding up between her cheeks above the tan line of her bikini, the point where everyone's eyes had previously been turned back briefly exposed now. Her head turned, her face flushed and mouth open, her eyes wide and wild, like a cat in high beams: he was catching up. And when he did catch up she would be in the backseat or on the side of the road, her back pressed against the ground, her breath taken away by the weight of his body, all her mother's clothing, so carefully sewn together, made well enough for her daughter's children to wear as costumes of a previous era, lying in shreds, and her face tied in a knot, biting her lower lip, eyes pulled into her skull, as he lowered himself.

In our minds love had gone bad, but not in theirs. "No," she said, pushing off his chest. "Not here. I want it to be perfect." He didn't understand, though he obeyed her, and she pulled him back against her on the seat where they lay together, her lips traveling over his face. "Just hold still," she said. "I always knew," she said, "it would be like this." He didn't know what *it* was or what *this* was, only that he had been chosen. He closed his eyes as she pressed his face against her sweater. All he could smell was her. "I love you," she said again and again until the sound of her voice covered him like a blanket. "I want to hear you say it." He said he had already said it, but she wanted him to say it again, so he did, repeating it into her sweater, into her breasts. "You do," she said, "don't you?"

She told him to hold his hands at his sides no matter what she did. He smiled at her, as if she was kidding. You trust me, she said. It was a question. He nodded in a way that made her love him even more. He was her child. He asked her what was the matter. Her eyes had watered. She told him nothing and ran her hand over his eyelids, smoothing them closed. "Hold still." He nodded. "You nodded!" she scolded and he tried not to smile. She sat on his lap, feeling her shorts ride up. She ran her finger along his forearm. His fingers twitched. Abruptly she laid her palms flat against his chest and pushed, angling her chin up. She took one shoulder in each hand and ran her hands down his arms as if she were wringing out wet clothes. He grinned. "Stop that!" she said. She undid her blouse and bra then put one hand on his shoulder, one against the side of his cheek, and lowered her chest against his face wrapping her arms around the back of his head. He raised his hands, she pushed them back down; he raised them again, she took them and sat on them. "There," she said. She leaned forward, pulling his nose between her breasts, his mustache tickling her skin, and found the edge of his knuckle between her legs.

They rocked together as if in an embrace of grief until her breaths came in quick, panicked bursts, as if she was short of breath, not him. She squeezed the back of his head so tightly he yelled into her chest. She rolled off him, backing against the far door, pulling her blouse over her chest. Her face was scrunched up, smeared.

"Don't tell anyone what happened," she mumbled.

His mind raced for something to say, not the wrong thing. "What?" he said. "What happened?"

She shook her head. "I don't know," she said. Whatever had happened it wasn't his fault. It was hers. She was cold. The windows had steamed up but were now frosted over. "It's all right," she said thinking of the movies, TV. It had all gone just like that until now. She tried to think of what would happen next. "I'm scared," she said, trying to follow the script. "Hold me." He moved over on the seat. Already, part of her didn't want him to touch her, but this couldn't be true.

She knew when she fell in love with him that she would be in love forever just as she knew when she woke up in the backseat the next morning, cramped and headachy, and looked at Dion sleeping with his mouth open that she was no longer in love with him and never would be. She opened the door and stepped out into the damp morning air. She began to think of Ron's long fingers resting on the steering wheel of his father's Mercury, his thin legs and gray slacks as they drove to the movies and held hands in the dark. She thought of his thin lips brushing against hers, his hand resting carefully on her shoulder, and of his parents reading in bed waiting for him to come home, his father's air-conditioning.

Dion stretched, scrunching his eyes, his limbs snaking around the corners of the seats up to the back dash. His T-shirt pulled up to show his stomach. He opened his eyes and watched her standing in the open doorway. He smiled.

"We should go," she said. "I'm afraid someone will find us here." He shrugged. Obviously he cared nothing for what people thought. How had she missed this before? He moved like an oaf, like her father, slowly opening the door, as if there was no hurry. Digging the keys out of his pocket. Finally he started the car and launched them forward, speeding. At least they were moving; she rolled the window down and stuck her face into the breeze as if into a splash of water. Poor Ron. What was he doing now?

"I'm not feeling well," she said, making a show suddenly of holding her stomach.

He leaned forward over the wheel and shot her a glance. "What's wrong?"

"I don't know," she said irritably, as if it was all his fault. He recoiled a little against his door and leaned his elbow out the window, steering with one thumb.

As they neared her house, he started to get nervous, leaning forward over the wheel.

"When am I going to see you again?"

She looked at the dashboard as if she hadn't heard. He pulled over to the side of the road and turned to her, the words she had been saying—his own name, and *I love you, I love you*—playing through his head. He wasn't going to say them, they were her words, and he didn't want to tell her to say them, but he needed her to keep saying them.

She put her hand on the door. He watched it resting there. "I can walk from here," she said and stepped out of the car.

"Where are you going?" He screamed so loudly she stumbled off the road. She could see her house from here, across the road and down the field.

"I don't love you anymore."

He was out of the car now with his hands on the roof, just looking at her.

She repeated it. Her bellow drew out and continued as a groan as she bent over with her knees together and hands pulled around her stomach. Tears burst down her cheeks, her blonde strands sticking to her lips.

It seemed now that he must have known all along what would happen. He could have made a noise like the sudden roar of gravel pouring from a dump truck at the construction site where his father worked. This much force and more had built up in his chest. He could have crushed her words with his own. He could have screamed so loudly she would have ceased to exist, but he was silent.

She sensed him stumbling through the field after her. Her mother came to the window, saw her, and called her father who arrived at the window with his shotgun. Seeing her father, Natalie ran away from the house toward the woods. Her mother came out onto the front steps and screamed, "Natalie!" Natalie tripped and vanished into the blonde straw. By the time she stood, her father was on the phone, calling. His friends ran for their trucks and cars, funneling from Central Street, Winthrop Road, and Water Street onto Litchfield Road.

Dion tripped on a log and twisted his ankle. She was out of sight. These were her woods; she had grown up playing here. He stood with his arms apart, hunkered down, and screamed her name as loud as he could.

She stopped running and looked up at the sky washing over the treetops. They could probably hear her name all the way in Bath, she thought. He loved her, he really did. She ran on, but stopped when her name sounded again and again, moaning through the trees like a foghorn, his voice seeming more desperate and distant. He was headed in the wrong direction. She almost called out to him.

Mr. Dawson opened his door and stepped out before putting his truck in park; it lurched forward slightly before he could hit the brake. No one was watching. His neighbor, Mr. Shumaker, ran across the lawn, taking long, even strides. Their boots crunched over the dried leaves and grass with the sound of falling water; all of them headed toward Natalie's father standing at the edge of the woods. "This way," he called and ran into the shadows. They all stopped running when Dion's voice called for Natalie. His voice, her name. They leaned over their knees, listening to their own heavy breathing. The smell of their own musty heat escaped from beneath their shirt collars.

A few of them had guns. He stopped calling her name. She turned at the edge of Nason's field when she heard the silence. When she listened harder she heard the voices of her father, her uncles, their friends, and the fathers of her friends calling to one another. For a moment she wanted to take it all back. She did love him. Then she wanted to take it all the way back to never having loved him to begin with. She couldn't say now how it had started. Ron would never forgive her. No one would.

They caught up with him, all the men shouting at once, stumbling and waving. Dion couldn't hear what any one of them said, only fragments of words and phrases. Finally Natalie's father appeared and Dion could see the resemblance in the shape of his face, thin but sagging near the jowls. Her father was the only one not shouting as the rest formed a circle around him, the ends of their waving gun barrels like dark eyes. Dion raised his hands as the police had told him to one night in Monmouth. He closed his eyes and pictured the house he and Natalie were going to have, every room smelling of her wrist, the bed with the tent, and the red barn with the horse, the boat with the captain taking them down the coast toward the sun. He could see it all so clearly it seemed as if these things had already happened and he was looking back now after a lifetime together.

"David Dion." It was her father's voice rising above the others. The father had a right to speak. He was the one wronged; anything he did might be excused later. Dion looked briefly at her father and the others. Her father's eyes darted around the woods, skipping off Dion's face every few seconds. Dion lowered his chin and closed his eyes again, holding his arms out so they would know he was unarmed. It seemed he had been waiting his entire short life to accept blame. "David Dion." His name again, and the picture Dion had formed on the backs of his closed lids of her father pointing a finger at him, eyes red with anger, almost with tears, was more accurate than the real thing. Dion waited for his name, imagining her father's mouth opening, his jagged teeth bared. Instead there was the deafening crack of a shotgun blast, and in the total silence that followed Dion found himself floating in the treetops, uncertain if he was dreaming or dying. The maple and oak leaves turned toward him and shivered. He saw the field beyond the woods where a burst of wind sliced a path through the grass like an invisible hand combing through hair. At the edge of the field near the road Natalie stood looking back. She made him so sad he had to look away, into the sun. When he looked back down it was too late: the image of the sun was burned into everything he saw.

I was outside our house throwing a tennis ball against the wall, pretending I was the star of a baseball game with scouts ready to sign me up, and was just winding up for another pitch when I heard the crack of the gunshot echo across town. My mother flew out the back door and grabbed hold of me, searching my arms and chest to see if I had been hit.

Mrs. Dawson dropped a sandwich roll at Dawson's, ran outside with the customers, and looked up at the sky. Natalie's mother fell to the floor in her kitchen. In her mind they were all dead: her husband, her daughter, and Dion. The police chief stood up from his desk and looked at the receptionist. He had been afraid of what might happen if people took the law into their own hands. This was the consummation of our relief.

When Dion opened his eyes he was still there, kneeling before his accusers, handfuls of dirt and pebbles sprinkled over his shoulders. All the men's eyes searched his body for wounds or blood, but there were none. Natalie's uncle had fired his shotgun by accident, blowing a hole in the ground and kicking up a cloud, nothing more.

Gazing back across the field to the woods where he lay dying, Natalie found it impossible to accept at first that they had shot him. But then it made sense, and she decided she would bear the mark of his death by never smiling again for the rest of her life. For her, the siren approaching from across town was the sound of an ambulance arriving too late, the second siren, which came a moment later, the sound of the police coming for her. She raised her chin and removed the strands of hair from her face to see if Dion's soul was rising out of his body over the treetops and into the sky. In court, as in her prayers to him, she would beg for mercy, for pardon. She would admit everything, absolving everyone but herself. For a few moments this morning she had been a fool thinking love was not real, thinking she could live without him, and now she had lost everything.

TREES

Lucy lay awake past midnight worrying about what she would bake the next day. She had tried everything from cakes to cheese breads, but her nephew Robbie only nibbled at the food she put out for his Wednesday visits.

In the morning, she made a batch of oatmeal cookies and set them on the rack to cool. Robbie nibbled at a few and looked through the window to the back field and the forty acres of woods sloping down to the river.

"You see the crowns on the spruce," he said, and she leaned over her steaming coffee to look. It was late spring, the ground had started to dry out and harden, and the field before the woods had started to green.

"They've topped out," Robbie said. "And that oak, see, it's getting in the way of those bird's eye maples. Now those maples, Aunt Lucy, they'd be worth something."

She nodded, as she always had when he talked about the need to thin and space. "Manage," he called it.

"A lot of people think all you do with the woods is let it grow," he said. "There's a lot more to it than that. They think it's a place to hunt deer or fool around in, a place to get in trouble."

"People are poaching in the woods?" she said. Her husband had hated poachers, and she thought of what else her nephew had just said—people fooling around? "Are they in there at night?"

"No, Aunt Lucy. I didn't mean people in *your* woods. I mean the woods in general, people in general."

"Oh, I see," she said, though she definitely didn't understand what he was talking about, and it made her nervous.

"I didn't mean to make you nervous, Aunt Lucy."

"No," she said. "Of course not."

"I just wanted to talk about your woods," he said and took a bite from one of her cookies.

The woods he referred to had belonged to her husband, also named Robert, and when she died, they would belong to her nephew. It made perfect sense: she and Robert never had children, and the farm had belonged to her husband's father and his father's father, and all the way back. Nevertheless, Robbie, her nephew, was always careful to say, "your woods." He was kindhearted, she knew, but she preferred he not talk about the trees. They would be his soon, and she thought that should be enough.

After her husband died five years before, her nephew began his weekly visits. Robbie's mother, Rebecca, had pushed him to come over. He was only a teenager then with no thoughts whatsoever about the future. They had little to talk about until he started dating Melanie and bringing her with him for his visits. Lucy loved Melanie—she was saucy and full of beans—but in the last two years she had stopped coming because she worked a half hour away in an old folks home. They called them something else now, but that's what it was. Lucy understood—Melanie was tired in the evenings, and busy on the weekends. She admired Melanie for getting out there and working. Robert had never wanted her to work, even when they were short on money. It was a point of pride with him but it was more than that, too. He had always wanted to protect her.

Robbie came by every Wednesday when he was in town even though he was also busy. In the late spring and summer, he worked at his father's lumberyard; in the winter, he worked in the woods cutting for a big operation that sold to Great Northern. Now Robbie and Melanie were in their twenties. They were thinking about the future.

"Actually, I've been meaning to talk to you about the trees," Robbie said, pulling his facial features into a knot. "I'm worried, you know, that the good trees got no room to grow and that some of the dead ones, specially them old spruce, they've got to be a fire hazard."

Robbie squeezed his eyes shut and rubbed his nose, just as her husband had done when he was trying to bring up a subject that made him nervous.

"I was thinking—Melanie and I were—that I should do some work down there for you. Before things get too bad and it's not worth anything. We can both make some money on it, you know."

It made her feel awful, this idea that something was wrong down in her husband's woods. People down there at night, hunting, starting fires.

"Robert loved those woods." She shook her head.

"He looked after them, but you can't be expected to, Aunt Lucy."

"You do an awful lot of work for me already, Robbie, and you never let me pay you."

"Now don't you worry about that," he said. "I'm worried, though, that Uncle Robert never spaced in there, and now everything's growing wild. I'm not saying Uncle Robert did the wrong thing. But he wasn't thinking about it, you know, toward the end. He was in no shape then to thin and space on his own and to take out what's valuable while it was worth something."

"He loved to sit out there in the woods by himself in the afternoon."

"Course he did. Uncle Robert had an eye for lumber like no other woodsman I ever knew. The man could spot heart rot from looking at the bark."

Lucy squeezed her fingers around her coffee spoon. There was something she wanted her nephew to understand about her husband. Robbie faced her, a simple and pleasant expression on his handsome face. She had known him as a baby.

"No one knew how to manage a forest like Uncle Robert," he said.

"But I don't think he wanted to *manage* it, as you say."

"I know, he was too old in the end, and I should've been around more to help him. He never woulda let it get so bad if I was here to help. I blame myself."

"No, Robbie, no. . . ."

"I know it's my fault, Aunt Lucy. I was too busy working up north. Right before Uncle Robert got sick I was trying to earn enough money to get a truck. Now we're trying to save enough to get married and buy a house. But it's always a busy time, Aunt Lucy, and I shoulda come by more often then."

"No, Robbie, you have your own life to live. You do enough for me as it is."

She was thinking how he had painted the house that summer and mown the field with his father's bush hog.

"Melanie and I are talking about having children."

"Oh, that's wonderful, Robbie. That makes me so happy to hear." And it did make her happy, the idea that someday children would live in this house.

"Don't tell my mother and father yet. They'll have all kinds of worries. You know them. But I thought I'd tell you."

"I'm so excited for you. I do wish you'd bring Melanie by sometime. I miss seeing her."

"We will, we will. She's so busy now, you know."

She meant to say she understood, but somehow she couldn't.

Robbie pushed his coffee away and stood up.

"I have to get back to the yard, Aunt Lucy."

"Yes," she said. "Of course you do."

"But I'm glad we agree on the woods. I'll come by tomorrow."

"Good," she said.

Through the kitchen window, she could see the wind moving through the upper branches of the trees at the edge of the field.

Lucy and Robert tried for years to have children. Each time she miscarried, there was more damage to her body until the doctors said it was no use. In the early years, Robert went into the woods in the fall and didn't come back until the spring thaw brought the logs down on the river drive. Later, he drove home some week-ends and on holidays unless they were snowed in. He never cut in his own woods behind the house. "It's money in the bank," he said once. His father had never cut back there either, except the oak cut down to make the banister and the pines cut down to frame the barn when the old one burned down. Otherwise, no one had cut in those woods since the lumber was taken out to build the house two hundred years ago just after the Revolution. Robert talked of little else in his last days, when it took him more than half an hour to make his way across the field leaning on her arm. Each generation had saved these woods, in case they were needed in the future. Going way back, he said, the really big spires were taken for masts, and a good deal of the white oaks for ribs, but after that, nothing. Not since we have lived here, he said. By "we" he meant his family, the Parkers.

After he stopped working, Robert would walk slowly across the field to spend several hours every afternoon in the woods sitting by himself under the thick canopy of leaves. Occasionally, she helped him, but she understood that he was accustomed to his life away from her in the woods, and she spent that time deciding what they would have for supper.

All his life her husband had been built like a tree himself, as straight and hard as the logs he skidded out of the woods north of Millinocket, a part of Maine she had never seen, even though he had spent more time there than he had with her. After he could no longer physically do the work in the camps and he came home for good, she thought finally she would have all of him. When he started spending his afternoons sitting in the woods down by the river, she realized there was a part of him she would never touch. Maybe it wouldn't have bothered her as much if they had been able to have children.

Once, Robert came back, hung his cane in the closet (he could still walk on his own then), and sat down at the kitchen table.

"I guess I worked hard enough," he said, "that we won't have to cut the trees down." He faced the field and the woods beyond, but his eyes were closed and his jaw slack as if in sleep.

In the last few years of his life, he collapsed inward, his knees and back barely strong enough to carry him from one side of the property to the other. Part of her was grateful then, for she finally had him entirely to herself. He was like a child. He needed her for everything. She helped him to the tree line and turned around while he struggled ten or twelve feet into the shade of the giant white oaks and maples. Those were the happiest times of her life.

After he was gone, she took over the habit of his vigil by sitting in the woods for an hour each afternoon on a bench he had hewn from a fallen hemlock. "Hemlock never rots," he had said. She thought of their life together. He had never wanted to talk about his winters working in the woods. It must have been cold, she guessed, sleeping in the uninsulated camps, fifty cots surrounding the wood stove. Days so cold the trunks of the pines cracked, sounding through the woods like gunshots. Her father had told her stories.

She had always known her husband lived two lives: one in the north woods, and one here on the farm with her.

After lunch, she walked down to the woods. She felt closer to him here, and as she gazed at the bark and leaves and needles, and at the green above spread like a blanket between her and the sky, the names of the trees came back to her: hemlock, white birch, red maple, white pine. Some of the pines seemed as wide as her car was long. Where the woods met the field, apple trees had gone wild, the tangled branches arching to the ground.

She was sitting at the kitchen table at ten in the morning the day after Robbie's usual visit when a knock sounded at the door. It was Robbie smiling in the window. She couldn't understand at first why he was here. It wasn't Wednesday, she hadn't baked anything. An older man she had never seen before nodded at her once and stared at his feet.

"We're going to be down the hill, Aunt Lucy. You won't even see us."

"Down the hill?" she said.

"Don't you remember, we talked yesterday?"

"Yes, of course I remember."

"We'll just be down in the woods then," he said.

She wasn't exactly sure what was about to happen. They had talked about the woods, but they had talked about it many times before. She didn't understand how they had come to this point all of a sudden.

"I don't want you to worry, Aunt Lucy. From up here, you won't even notice the difference. We got a whole crew down there. Only take a few days."

She nodded and looked down at the two pairs of boots on the doorstep.

"Now there's a bit of money in it for you, Aunt Lucy."

"I don't need the money."

"Of course you do. You need a new roof. And the foundation is cracked on the south side."

He was probably right about these things. She had always kept the house clean and the garden weeded. She didn't know how much it cost to fix a cracked foundation or put on a roof. Her husband had taken care of all that. She needed to keep the house in good shape; someday it would belong to Robbie. To him and to Melanie. She had some money, she wanted to tell him, but didn't. She had always saved money, even when there was little to save.

At first she thought to bake something, in case Robbie and the other one came in for lunch—they hadn't carried lunch pails with them—but when the chain saws started she had to sit down. It felt as if a screw was tightening the column of her spine, paralyzing each muscle. More than two buzzed down at the bottom of the slope. It sounded like an army. She sat there all morning until finally the buzzing stopped at noon and she walked down the hall to the bathroom. The sound returned after lunch and lasted until dark when it stopped but still echoed through her thoughts all night, long after the boys had gone home, holding her on the edge of sleep. She woke up past eight to the sound of the saws already at work again. There seemed to be more of them today than the day before.

She dressed quickly, pulling her coat over her nightgown and hurrying out the door and down the road to Robbie's parents' house. Charlie wouldn't be home, but Rebecca, Robbie's mother, would be, and she would have to see that there had been some misunderstanding.

Rebecca answered the door and waved Lucy inside. Rebecca was on the phone so Lucy sat down and clamped her hands between her knees. The buzzing was loud, even this far away.

Rebecca leaned against the wall on the other side of the room. Lucy watched her lips move, but she couldn't hear what she said. The murmur of her voice sounded like the purring approval of a cat. Lucy hated to be reminded that she didn't like someone, but it was hard to avoid with Rebecca.

"I'm afraid I'm on my way out the door, Aunt Lucy," Rebecca said.

"It's just about the trees," she said.

"The trees?"

"Down the hill. Behind the house—they're cutting down the trees."

"I thought Robert talked to you. He told me that he talked to you, about the thinning."

"Yes, he did. He did."

"Then I don't understand what the matter is, Aunt Lucy. I'm going to be late."

"I'm sorry. I didn't mean to barge over like this."

"Well for goodness sake. If you talked to him—did he not tell you what he was going to do?"

"I didn't know he was going to cut the trees down."

"I'm afraid I just don't understand. He came over to talk to you about thinning. We told him he had to talk to you first."

"He did, yes, he did."

Rebecca looked at her watch.

"But I didn't know he was going to cut them down."

"Not all of them, for goodness sake. I don't know what you thought he was going to do."

"Robert—he was saving those trees."

"Saving them for what? They don't last forever. I'll talk to Robbie, and I'll have him go back over to see you, and you can tell him what your worries are. I may not see him tonight, though. I won't be back in time to tell him tonight. I've got a meeting. We're planning a sale at the library, and he goes to bed early."

Her nephew had everything, Lucy wanted to yell but stayed silent. He had Melanie. He had a new truck, he would have her land and her house filled with children and grandchildren. She and her husband had always saved everything. During the war, everyone did. Robert was in the war for four years, fighting his way from Sicily to Germany while his younger brother

Charlie, Robbie's father, came in at the very end to guard prisoners for six months. Robbie had no idea what it had cost her and her husband (and their parents who had provided through the Depression) to put off what they wanted and do with less.

In the morning, she left soon after the saws started, for a parish meeting. Afterward, Elsie had people over for tea and coffee. Elsie had a big house on the opposite side of Vaughn, and though Lucy was too distracted to listen to the other women, at least she couldn't hear the saws. She stayed as long as she could and afterward went to the town landing to look out at the river until the sun went down. They couldn't work in the dark.

The next morning, Robbie stood on the front step with the low light at his back, his face in the shadow.

"Aunt Lucy? Hello," he said, his voice just like her husband's. She sat down at the kitchen table, the breath taken out of her.

"My mother said you came over about the woods. She said you were worried we would leave a mess or something."

He went to the cupboard, pulled out a glass, and filled it with tap water.

As if he already owns the place, as if I'm already dead, she thought but then felt guilty. She offered him some juice or some coffee.

"No, water's good. Thank you, Aunt Lucy."

She put the pot on anyway.

"I want you to know you can rest easy," he said. "Uncle Robert would be proud of the job we're doing down there. Uncle Robert was a real woodsman, last of the old guys. He liked a job done clean at the end, and that's the way we're gonna leave it, don't you worry."

"I'm not worried about that."

"We're leaving some four inch and smaller—new growth."

"Yes, yes, I'm sure you are." Her eyes began to burn, and she squeezed them shut to keep from crying. "You see, I'm worried about the trees—the trees, you know, Robert. . . ."

"Uncle'd be very happy with the job. Very happy, Aunt Lucy. I don't want you to worry. We won't send nothing to pulp. Mostly logs, mostly logs, even in the spruce, and not really cause of the money. Uncle woulda wanted it that way. He hated things going to pulp. But the thing he'd be wild over, Aunt Lucy, is this birdseye maple we got. Gonna make beautiful cabinets in some rich guy's kitchen. No, you don't have to worry about a thing."

The saws continued after he left. She dressed quickly in front of the mirror, her hands hurrying around her waist. She put on her long brown coat, packed her pocketbook in her purse, and held the keys in her hand, ready to walk down the front steps. It wouldn't do any good to go to any of the women she knew from church, the wives of her husband's friends, whom she had known for years. Her friends. They would listen, maybe a few of them would understand, but they were all busy with families of their own. They couldn't do anything. The only person she could think of going to was someone most people didn't think of as a very good person at all—Don Small, who had once owned the garage in town. She had not thought of him in years, but she felt he was the only one who could help her.

Don's life had not been easy. One of his children had spent time in prison after causing quite a bit of trouble in Vaughn and somewhere else. Don and his wife had lived apart after the birth of their second child. His wife—Lucy could picture her round face but could not remember her name—died of cancer when the children were still young. The poor children went to live with their grandmother while Don stayed above the garage on Water Street. She had heard that he now lived way out the Litchfield Road before the old MacRitchie farm, in what one of her friends described as the remains of an old shack. She had heard that news three years ago and she didn't know, as she drove out of the valley, if he would still be there or if he was even alive anymore. He would be older than her by a few years.

Twenty years ago during a winter of heavy snow, her old Pontiac began to spew black smoke out of the tailpipe on her way back from Boyton's Market. If Robert had not been working in the woods, he would have fixed the car himself. She brought it to Don

Small, who had already closed his shop for the day. It was dark, the snow spiraling in the streetlight. She had to knock on the door to his upstairs apartment. He was bleary eyed. Maybe he had already started drinking, but he was courteous, calling her ma'am. They lived in the same town, but they had never spoken before. He had a boy manning the pump during the day, and he rarely came out of the garage to talk to anyone. He told her the car wasn't fit to drive. After some protest, she accepted a ride home in his truck. He put her groceries in the back under a tarp. The snow stopped and it was a clear crisp night, the banks towering and the powder of the fields crystalline in the moonlight. They didn't speak all the way up the hill. He helped carry in the groceries and stood mute in the dark house with his long arms hanging at his sides.

They were together that once, that one night, and to her knowledge no one saw him leave before dawn. She told him they could never see each other again, and he looked at her from the shadow of the doorway to the bedroom and didn't answer.

For years he called, always when Robert was away. She knew it was him because no one spoke when she said hello. She lived in fear that someone would find out or that Don would come to the house and force himself inside. He never did; he just called and hung up, like a teenager. She felt when he called how much he wanted her and thought about her in ways that her husband never had. On many Sundays, she asked for forgiveness but never of the priest. She was afraid of what he would think, of the look he would have on his face every time she saw him on Sunday or at the market. She never felt forgiven, though she did, eventually, feel less guilty. In the end, she wasn't certain she wanted to be forgiven. She had traveled that night with Don to the very edge of the known world. She had wanted to see just once what it would feel like to throw everything away, and over the years she had wished on several occasions that Don would tell everyone and slash through everything she knew.

The secret they shared had, over time, earned him a mythical power in her mind. No one, however, not even Don, could take away what had never been given by her own marriage, by her own body. And, in the end, she didn't want to lose what she did have. Her years with Robert were all she had. Each time Don called, the silence on the other end of the line was the sound of Robert, her friends, the priest, and the parish vanishing into the ether of pure white snow. After he finally stopped calling, though, she felt emptiness inside her that she hadn't noticed before.

She was here at Don's house (if you could call it a house, with a hole in the roof and half the windows boarded over) to ask his help in saving the last of what she had feared losing: the trees her husband had loved maybe more than he had been able to love her.

The man in the doorway didn't look familiar, though it was Don. He was shorter, much shorter, hunched, and his dry cheeks had faded into a delicate onion skin. He wore a stiff blue cap, which he took off and quickly put back on again, and he made a grunting noise—not quite a greeting—before backing away from the door, leaving it open. She wasn't sure she wanted to go inside, but she did, and removed a metal object the size and shape of a fist (some part of a car, she guessed) from a wooden chair before sitting down. Don sat on a filthy old couch and turned his head to the side, as if he expected someone to come out of the next room.

She started talking frantically about the woods behind the house. "The trees," she said. "My nephew's cutting them all down. I know he is. They were my husband's trees." She described what kind they were, or what kind she thought they were—hemlocks, pines, maples. She didn't know what to do to stop her nephew, she said. She had asked him to stop, or at least she thought she had asked him to stop. She went on longer than she intended to, describing how her husband had loved the trees and never wanted them to be cut. Finally, with all her will, she stopped herself from talking and saw that Don wasn't listening—he couldn't listen. His eyes, staring right at her, were like small green stones in a clear brook. The same thing had happened to Robert before he died.

She looked around and saw an old cot in the corner and piles of opened cans on a crumbling sink counter. Flies buzzed above a mound of half-filled trash bags.

For some reason, he had stuffed some of the cans into the wood stove. The stench was overwhelming now, and the worst of it was the smell of urine coming from his filthy pants. He looked down at his hands (which alone remained unchanged after more than twenty years) and back up at her.

"Oh, Don," she said, and his face softened into a smile almost of recognition. While Don sat in his old chair looking from his hands, to her, and back to his hands, she carried trash bags full of cans and rotting food scraps out to the road. She pumped water into a bucket, and scrubbed the floor and the counters. Finally, she hand washed what clothes she found in cardboard boxes, and hung them to dry on a rope she tied from a branch to the shell of an old porch light next to the front door. Don watched her work for the rest of the day. It was late afternoon when she finished, the sun low in the trees when she squeezed Don's hand to say goodbye, and he looked up at her to smile again. Someone had been coming by to drop off food for him— some distant kin, probably—but they were doing little else. Don stood on his stoop and waved once as she backed out of the drive.

Tomorrow she would call Elsie, she thought, as she drove up the hill. Elsie would help him. She had worked in hospice care in Augusta and was now in charge of a group of women from the parish who looked after old people who had no one else. Of course,

Lucy would have to explain why she was at Don's in the first place, and she wasn't a good liar.

She entered her house and put her bag down on the table before she heard the absence of the saws buzzing down the hill. Maybe they had quit early. As she walked along the trail behind the house to the woods, she thought about what she would say to Elsie, and all the women in the congregation Elsie would talk to about how Lucy had started doing old Don Small's laundry. She could say she was just driving by and saw what a state the place was in, but driving by on the way to where? She could say she had heard he needed help, but heard from whom? Who would talk to her about the old mechanic who had once lived above his shop where he drank and befriended no one? She decided she wouldn't explain anything. Damn them all. She would tell Elsie there was a man out Litchfield Road before the MacRitchie place, who lived alone and needed help. She wouldn't even name him. She would tell Elsie that no one should die dirty and all alone. It lacked any dignity at all. In fact, she would volunteer to go down there herself and check on him once or twice a week.

Lucy followed the path through a thin wall of trees into the open light. Except for a few spindly birches and maples, no wider than her calf, all the trees had been cut down on the hill that sloped to the river. Long-armed branches lay strewn waist high around stacks of sixteen-foot logs, reminding her of a photograph she had seen of a field of fallen soldiers. The vast maze, so dense that it had seemed impenetrable, was now bare and washed by the sun. She leaned against the butt end of an old pine, the still damp wood staining her fingers with sap. It would take a lifetime— more than a lifetime—for the trees to grow as tall again. No one now living would survive to see them cover the sky. She had always known that her nephew would cut them down, but she had hoped that he would wait until she was gone. It seemed so little to ask, she thought, just to wait.

THE PLAINS OF ABRAHAM

I belonged to a large family that had lived in the same town in Maine for over two hundred years. When those who had moved away came back in August to visit, we treated them as if they had never left, and in some ways they hadn't. No matter where they had moved to or what they had done with their lives, they still looked and acted like Ingersolls, at least while they were among us. Even those we called married-ins seemed to acquire the tense Ingersoll jaw and the officious presence that I have only otherwise noticed in school crossing guards and the managers of fast food restaurants.

Our family had never been wealthy or influential (our ancestors first came to Vaughn to farm for the original Vaughn family), but we liked to think we were intelligent and sturdy, if nothing else, as evidenced by our determination to stay in one place for such a long time. We also liked to think that we had always, from the beginning, come down on the right side of things, even when it was dangerous to do so. A distant uncle, a deacon of Newbury, spoke out against the witch trials while they were happening, not afterward when it was safe. Half a dozen of us died fighting King Phillip's men; one Ingersoll actually reached Quebec with Arnold on his treacherous winter expedition (though it's never been clear, to me at least, what that says about us); another defied our employer, the founders of the town, to oppose the English during the Revolution; another refused to serve on ships involved in the rum trade, choosing instead to work in the woods for a fraction of the pay.

After my grandfather's death, my father became the head of our clan; he was the oldest living member of the family still in Vaughn, and for forty years he had taught history in the local high school. When he retired from teaching, he announced that he would throw a party for himself that he said would double as a family reunion. He hired an old boom towing barge converted into a tour boat to take us on an evening cruise across nearby Lake Sumner, where my great grandfather had built a log cabin. When I was young, my grandfather had maintained a raft with a diving board at the old camp, and my brother, cousins, and I had spent hours there swimming and warming our pale skin in the August sun. The lake was always cold, even in the middle of summer.

On the day of the party, more than a hundred extended family members and old friends climbed the gangway and mingled in the cool breeze of a mild summer evening. August is the only time of year in Maine when the weather could be called ideal. The mosquitoes and black flies had taken a break and the air seemed braced for the coming fall. The tips of the spruce rocked in the reflection of the water, and the hills to the west balanced in the haze of the horizon. My mother and I leaned over the railing on the top deck and talked about what their lives would be like now that my father wasn't working. I thought they should travel somewhere, but she said nothing much would change. He would volunteer in the schools up and down the valley, and she would continue at the school library.

After my mother went down to the first deck to find my father, my brother Henry jumped out of an old Chevy that had pulled into the parking lot, thanked the driver for a ride, and boarded just as the captain was about to cast off. No one had expected my brother—he hadn't been home in more than ten years—and I don't think anyone else noticed him. Though he had a beard and dark shaggy hair now, he still moved with the same rolling gait. As we headed out into the lake, I tried to make my way toward him at the back of the boat, but it had been years, in some cases, since I had seen certain cousins and aunts who lived out of state, either in New Hampshire or Vermont, and others, too—friends of my parents from Vaughn, old teachers, my father's buddies. I visited Vaughn twice a year but only briefly.

My mother accosted me in a minor frenzy and asked me to come down to the lower deck and help at the food table. People were making a mess, she said. By then, I couldn't spot Henry, and I began to wonder if I had seen him at all.

Clouds swept over just before sunset and then it was pitch black in the middle of the lake. The former high school principal put his arm around my father and leaned forward to tell some anecdote to a small circle of people. I knew all the stories about my father: there was the time he leapt out of the classroom window to make some point. I couldn't remember what. Another time he made everyone eat hard tack and several students had to go home sick. No one ever complained. He convinced the conservative school board that he didn't need to have any tests in his U.S. history class. He gave his own kind of tests, often outdoors, where students were asked to reenact certain events and speak in the voice of important figures. Field tests, he called them.

I tried to get my mother to settle down and mingle, but she darted around the food, replacing finger sandwiches and cheese. Brendan Lee (head of the Maine Board of Education under two governors and my father's old roommate from Orono) brought the party to order by tapping his wine glass.

"I wish I could say we were all here just to have a good time," he said. "But alas, school must begin, and today we have a history lesson on the history teacher himself. Can we blame him for Old Vaughn Day, that rowdy mess that takes place on Water Street every July? And that green park down by the river? Yes, we can. Would the high school have lost its accreditation ten years ago if this man had not devoted hundreds and hundreds of hours to drawing up the changes that made the difference? The man to blame for all these catastrophes stands right over there. We all know him. Everyone knows him. He was born here and for forty years he has taught in the same classroom.

"Jack and I were roommates together up at Orono—before the Civil War. I remember thinking then that this guy could do *anything* he wanted to in life, and he chose to come back here, to Vaughn, and teach history to the children of this town. He could not have chosen a worthier path. His kingdom was his classroom, but he has been a leader to all of us who have known him."

Brendan Lee stepped aside for my father to say a few words. My father waved him off at first but Brendan said, "I think we could all do with one more lesson."

My father smiled and bowed his head, trying to pretend, I knew, that he hadn't rehearsed what he was about to say.

"Anyone who has taken one of my classes knows that the word 'lesson' is second only to 'wisdom' in my lexicon of useless words. But here I am. I am a freshman again, without lessons, leaving the life I have

known, the school I have known, for the unknown."
He paused, head bowed, lips pursed, and then he said
something that I could tell he had not planned to: "The
trouble with teaching," he said, "if you're any good at it,
is that you never grow older than your students." He
looked up, surprised at his own words, and before he
could move on, my brother stepped out of the crowd
behind me and edged along the wall. My father and
brother eyed each other for a moment until my brother
reached for the handle of a door I had not noticed and
stepped out into the darkness. There was a splash, and
then we were all quiet listening to the ambient hum of
the engine beneath us. My mother ran forward into the
space between my father and his audience and turned
in a circle.

"What?" she said. She whirled around, looked frantically over my face and chest as if for signs of injury,
and turned to my father. "Henry!" she yelled. "Did I see
Henry?" The second call for her son sent everyone into
action. My father came forward to comfort her, but she
hit him hard in the chest and pushed him away.

Jim, the photographer from the *Valley Journal*, who
had been quite a few years younger than me in school
and an only child, did what I should have done and
flung himself out into the lake with all three of his
cameras wrapped around his neck. Doug Molloy, a kid
I had known in school, and now the new history
teacher, technically my father's replacement, followed,
hitting the water in his sport coat and with his wine

glass still fixed in his hand. One of my father's broth
ers jumped in, along with two of my cousins. I prepared
to go, too, taking off my jacket and my shoes and lay-
ing them next to the wall, but the captain pulled me
back.

"We don't need anyone else in the water," he said,
raising both his hands in the air.

"Why is there a door there?" Brendan Lee
demanded. My mother looked at the open door in disbelief, but it was the opening we had walked through
when we climbed the gangway to board the boat earlier in the evening. Of course, someone should have
locked it.

The captain returned to the helm and told everyone
through the intercom that all parties would be rescued.
The boat turned around and the crew searched the
water with spotlights. My father and mother stood in
the bow on the upper deck, calling Henry's name. I felt
there was little I could add to the situation now and sat
down on the lower deck next to a bottle of wine and a
plate of cheese. People huddled and discussed in
hushed tones what had happened. Occasionally, they
glanced at me—the brother, the son. I was used to
being one or the other in Vaughn, but I had not lived
in Vaughn for some time. The sound of my parents
calling for Henry rose above all the other voices.
Eventually, my father gave up and people around me
quieted down, leaving just the echo of my mother's
croaks.

The crew rescued the young teacher and the photographer, who had yanked off his cameras and shoes to save himself, and now seemed somewhat chagrined as they covered him with a blanket. They pulled my uncle and cousins out of the water. All of them had stripped off their shoes. Even as other boats joined the search, I never once considered that any harm had come to Henry. I had never believed anything could happen to him, but this was a belief forged in childhood, in the mind of a younger brother. Now he was a man who had been living out of a backpack for ten years.

Our boat returned to the dock, and people skulked off to their cars. I rode with a cousin to the house where my parents waited in the living room, each in their respective chairs, for some news. My father's two sisters waited in the kitchen with four cousins. They wanted to be on hand in case they were needed, but they didn't want to intrude on my parents' distress and grief, which they all would have considered a private matter.

Normally, my father, a member of the volunteer fire department for forty years, would have been out there helping, but I had heard someone say to him as we left the boat that he should see to my mother. He looked like the star athlete benched for the rest of the game, shocked and stunned that he was not indispensable. Finally, as the sun came up, my mother rose to make everyone breakfast, and I went over to stand by my father and gaze with him out the window at the black locust tree we had planted on my tenth birthday. The twenty-foot high branches were covered now with white blossoms.

History, our father was often fond of saying when Henry and I were young, is a mirror, though he would usually rejoin that he had not meant "mirror"—not exactly. "Not exactly" was his stock response to any pretense at certainty. For such a skeptic, though, he loved to speak in absolutes. He claimed it was a teaching method, a way of baiting his students (and as his children, my brother and I were always his students) onto thin ice. He used to make Henry and me watch an hour of TV a day—anything we wanted as long as it was "popular"—while he stood behind us attacking (in a steady monotone), the lies perpetrated on a comatose public. To prove we were comatose, he once held the hall mirror next to the TV so we could see ourselves watching.

Our father had very little tolerance for people who didn't understand right away, and even less tolerance for people who could understand if they wanted to, but showed no interest. He was never sure which category I fit into. I confused him, I think, by earning an A in French and a C- in social studies. Just when he had decided I was hopeless, I would do well. No sooner had he congratulated me on my success, than I would fail an exam. For a while, in junior high, he made me his project: my eraticism, he called it, was due to lack of discipline and inefficient method. He clocked my study hours at night and monitored my note taking. When my grades went down, he finally raised his voice at dinner one night, declaring that I just wasn't trying to focus. My mother stepped in (which she rarely did) and told him that was enough.

In a final effort to transform me, my father signed me up for the junior high basketball team because I was tall for the ninth grade. The coach, a friend of his, kept me after practice trying to improve my skills, and my father enlisted two of my older cousins, one of whom was on my team and one of whom was on the high school team, to help me with my ball handling. I made some progress at the free-throw line when no one else was in the gym, but the coach benched me for most of the first game until the last four minutes of the final quarter, when we were hopelessly behind. I ran up and down the court and managed to stand in the right places with my hands in the air. I could feel my father watching me intently, leaning forward in the bleachers with his chin in his hand. The unfortunate moment arrived when I found myself open, and someone passed me the ball. I saw it coming and raised my hands, but I miscalculated somehow and it thudded against my chest. The buzzer sounded, freezing everyone's eyes on me, and I saw my father, one hand extended up along his temple. I had expected to see disappointment and shame on his face, but not the kind of terror only a child can imagine, in which the smallest failure or embarrassment has the power to destroy.

It was a good thing, my mother said to me after the game, that my father had other things to focus on. He had Henry, and he had his book. For ten years, from when I was very young until just after Henry left, our father worked on a book about the Battle of the Plains of Abraham, *the* event, according to him, that had shaped the future of North America. He spent two hours after dinner every night behind the shut door of his small office at the back of the house supposedly working on the book, which no one knew about except my mother, Henry, and me. Through the keyhole, I watched his monolithic back expand with his slow breathing.

"If Wolfe had not seen the path on the side of the cliff into the Achilles' heel of Montcalm's defense," our father explained as we drove north to Quebec for one of our yearly visits to the Plains, "he would have been forced to attack head on up the steep bluffs, or go around the bend in the river to another fortified position. He had only a few days to attack before he would have to sail for England to avoid being iced in for the winter. If he had attacked head on, he would have lost the majority of his forces. Despite his corrupt mismanagement of the colony, Vaudrevil might have retained Canada for France; encouraged by the victory, Louis XVI might have reinforced his troops. England might have left New France alone and focused instead on

New England, possibly short-circuiting the American Revolution. Without the American Revolution, French troops would not have returned to help inspire the French Revolution—no Napoleon."

His eyes widened as he painted an alternate picture of our past, as if he were shaping its course with his own words.

The last trip we took to Quebec was the summer Henry turned sixteen and I turned thirteen. We had no radio, but our mother had an incredible memory for songs, which she belted out hour after hour in her off-key voice. My father sang along as well, as these were mostly the songs (Elvis, Buddy Holly, the Supremes) of their courtship, from a time before Henry and I were born. I hummed along, leaning into the front seat, while Henry sat back looking out the window. Or he slept. Even among his family, he was slightly aloof much of the time.

We stayed, as always, in a campground outside Quebec City, and at night around the fire my father reminded us of the history of the battle as the English General Wolfe faced it on September 13, 1759. He drew with a piece of kindling the rivers enclosing Quebec to the east. The Cap Rouge flowed between cliffs and high, wooded banks until it joined the St. Lawrence. The city was protected on all sides and should have been impenetrable, even to a superior force.

"Wolfe on one side, Montcalm on the other. Quebec a natural fortress. The Lower Town, houses, warehouses, and docks, lay along the riverside. The Upper Town perched atop the bluffs."

In the glow of the firelight, I watched shadows form in the lines of my father's face below his temples as he looked from one to the other of us. For the first time during the trip, my brother's attention sharpened.

"Maybe it was just chance that he saw the path," Henry said, and I knew he was only trying to get our father going.

"*No*, Henry," our father said. "Only someone of Wolfe's character could have noticed that. Steep cliffs two hundred feet high stretch unbroken for miles on either side of the city," our father continued, looking at Henry.

On the outside, our father said, Wolfe was the antithesis of a hero: a neurotic, diseased, secretive military fanatic. He suffered from severe depression and impenetrable silences followed by fits of yelling at his officers. He was short, ugly, and dying, just like his empire. But Wolfe (or someone in his command) spotted an inlet two miles west of Quebec with an overgrown path winding up the cliff face to a weak spot in the French defenses, and this made him a hero.

The next day we drove into Quebec and went straight to the Plains, a plateau about three-quarters of a mile wide, now surrounded by buildings, shops, houses, and steady traffic. My father played the role of the French Captain Vergor, dozing in his tent after having sent most of his militia home to gather in the crops. Henry played Wolfe's lead pathfinder. Branches and sticks served as our guns and knives. I had worried on the drive up that Henry might think he was too old for these games, now that he had a girlfriend, Michele, and was the star of the baseball team; but in the bushes by the cliff, he kneeled down and assumed his command. We both smeared mud on our faces, which our mother refused to do, though she had brought scarves for us to tie around our heads. She didn't seem to care that scarves were not period uniform for either side.

"Paul," Henry said to me, "You come up the left flank on my signal."

"Jo," he said, making our mother laugh. "You take the right flank."

"What's the signal?" I asked.

"A whip-poor-will call," he said, pressing his fingers to his lips and letting out a low trill. Henry pointed to the edges of the field to our left and right and then drew a map with his stick in the dirt, just as our father had done.

"You take out these two sentries," he said to me, "and Jo will take out two on the other side." Our mother laughed again.

Our father, meanwhile, reclined in his camp chair with his stick gun resting against his thigh and yawned before reloading his antique pipe. We took up our positions, and I mimicked cutting the throats of two sentries before looking to Henry to see if he was watching. He nodded approval and whistled. We all came creeping out of the bushes toward our father, who removed his pipe from his mouth and gawked with mock surprise as Henry and my mother tackled him to the ground. I tripped and then hung back, watching as my mother rolled away and Henry and our father continued wrestling. After he pinned our father, Henry took off running across the field toward Quebec with his stick raised in the air. His body sprung like a coil, his feet propelling through the grass. He wouldn't stop until he had taken the city.

"Come here," our mother said when she noticed me. "Come on, sit down," she said, reaching into her bag for our sandwiches. "The battle's over. Do you want turkey or roast beef?"

I turned from her and walked away to look over the bank to the river.

It took me a long time to understand that my father was incapable of focusing on more than one thing at a time, and when that one thing was not General Wolfe, it was Henry. After my failure on the basketball court, he could no longer see me most of the time. I wasn't there even when I stood right in front of him. Henry and my father were the same. When Henry was pitching, he told me, he couldn't hear people in the bleachers or calls from the other players. He didn't see the batter's face, just the catcher's glove. When he spoke to me, he focused in on me and heard every word I said, but as soon as we arrived at school or he saw one of his friends or one of our cousins or Michele, he pulled inside himself. He had a friendly way of standing erect and smiling in large groups that made him appear relaxed. I knew he wasn't.

I think I knew before anyone that my father was no longer working on his book when he locked himself in his room after dinner. I listened at the door, but did not hear the keys of his typewriter snap. Whatever energy he had once put into his project, he now poured into Henry. He monitored Henry's grades, proofread everything he wrote for school, attended practice, and talked with Henry about his pitching strategy over dinner every night. The more my father worked on him, the more Henry began to resemble a book. There was a purpose, a thesis, to each day: studying for a test, shaving imperfections off his fastball, gaining total control over the curveball.

I was the opposite of my father and Henry: I couldn't focus on any one thing—a sentence, a face, a math problem—for more than a couple seconds. In a crowd or a classroom or the basketball court, I took in all the peripheral information and almost never what I was supposed to focus on. Between the release of the basketball and its thud against my chest, I saw the anticipation on my father's face, the bored look of a girl sitting in the bleachers, and the clenched fist of the coach.

I spent most of my time looking out the second-story window of our house and daydreaming. I liked to imagine what life had been like in our town when our family first came there. My father had talked about our ancestors so much that I felt as if they were still among us, plowing fields and gathering firewood. At one time, when the slope of the valley from our doorstep to the riverbank was still a cow pasture, ages before any of us were born, our cape at the top of Central Street had been a farmhouse on the edge of town. The landscape had changed since 1750, though, and from my bed-room I could see all the buildings that had come up and the empty lots where a few had fallen. Sometime in the late 1950s, they tore down the old high school and built a modern flat-roofed school behind us that housed grades 7–12 and drew students from all the outlying farms and villages.

The Vaughn Woods, a piece of the old Vaughn farm the family opened to the town, that lay between our street and the new high school was the one place Henry and I spent any time alone away from the fam-ily and his friends. Except in the winter, when the snow was too deep, he and I walked the trail through the woods to school. The fields in the Vaughn Woods were arranged like a series of symmetrical rooms, each room a hay field separated by a strip of fir trees. In the spring after the ground had dried out, the warmth of the sun released the sweet smell of new grass sprouting from thawed mud. Our pace quickened in the cooler air of the shaded dales. Our mother called it our route through Arcadia, which I shared with his girlfriend Michele. They often walked back together after his practice, and I took the road home.

Sometimes Henry and I didn't talk the whole way to school; it didn't bother me. He went over his French grammar or recited chemistry formulas. He was second in the class, in his junior year, behind the vice principal's daughter. I just liked to be with him, and eventually I took on the job of quizzing him from note cards.

In the fall, Michele and I usually watched baseball practice from the fence that ran along the parking lot, and once I remember she said that Henry and I looked a lot alike. In a few more years, she said, when I grew, I would look just like him. I thought she was kidding at first; what she said made no sense.

"Sometimes I wish he was more like you, that's all." She looped her arm around mine and smiled at Henry who stood out on the field and paid no attention to us.

That afternoon I walked home with them through the Vaughn Woods. Much of the way the trail was wide enough for us to walk side-by-side, but it narrowed after the stone bridge over the stream, and I had to follow behind them listening to Henry talk about a test he had taken that day in chemistry. I stopped walking and listened as his voice trailed off and melded with the sound of the stream. They vanished around a bend, and though I wanted to catch up to them, I could not move. Michele's words played through my head and I wanted her to take it back.

Late in the fall of his senior year Henry pitched three consecutive no-hitters. It was the first time a team from Vaughn had ever won the state championship. The coach and my father started talking scholarship or minor league after a college scout showed up during one of the final games to clock his pitches. The scout spent most of his time outside the fence, watching each pitch, making occasional notes in a black book. He spoke only briefly to Henry.

I watched the last game from my perch up in a tree off the third-base line. Henry's expression never changed, his concentration never broke, and every time he rose over the pitcher's mound, I shut my eyes, and every time a batter struck out, I didn't think he could possibly throw another perfect pitch. Henry never flinched, though, and after the last batter struck out, the entire team rushed onto the field and lifted him into the air. They carried him over to the bleachers where the parents and most of the town were gathered.

Walking through Vaughn Woods on Monday morning, Henry and I relived every moment of the last inning, and when we pushed through the front doors of the school, kids rushed up to us, patting me on the back as well as him. That afternoon during a ceremony in the gymnasium, Henry walked across the floor to receive an achievement award sent from the governor himself, and I was reminded once again of how our paths in life would diverge. There had never been any question of Henry staying with us for long in Vaughn. Everyone, especially my father, had always spoken of him in terms of where he would go and how far he would rise. When the whole school stood and clapped, my father, on stage with the other teachers, buried his hands in his pockets and looked at the floor. At first I thought he was afraid someone would see pride in his face, but when he finally looked up, I saw the same fear that I had seen at my basketball game.

After the award ceremony, I waited for Henry outside the school. It took a long time for him to make his way through the crowd, and then he talked for a while with Michele and members of the team. I had seen Michele's mother, so I knew Henry wouldn't walk home with her. Even so, I knew I should have just gone on home alone—people had been coming up to Henry all day, and he looked tired. I wanted desperately to be alone with him, though, and to hear his voice talk about the different moments of the game—when the kid from Monmouth hit a foul that was almost a homer, when he almost walked their shortstop. I let him pass me and then I fell in behind him. With Michele and the others still watching, he turned around and yelled, "Will you for once stop following me around!"

He rushed around the corner of the school, and I followed him to the parking lot, empty now except for one car in the corner. Rod and Denny stepped out, careful not to slam their car doors, and followed Henry into the woods. I started to run—I knew a side path I could take to rush ahead and warn Henry—but then I stopped and let them go.

Rod and Denny dressed in jean jackets and cutoff T-shirts; they smoked in the parking lot and drove cars without mufflers. My father described them as just the kind of students who gave up on him without giving the class a chance, but actually they were just the kind of students our father gave up on the minute he saw them.

I walked home by the side of the road and was behind the house when Henry came out of the woods, limping slightly, holding his elbow. I thought maybe Rod and Denny had pushed him around a little, but I didn't think for a moment that they could have beaten him up. I waved, somehow feeling that he and I would be even now for what he had said to me. He didn't wave back, though, and the door slammed behind him. Everything was quiet. The smell of cut hay swelled in the air.

After the fight, as my father called it, Henry wouldn't get out of bed for a week, and he wouldn't talk to any of us. My father gave a speech, as my mother and I listened in the hall, on how there was no shame in taking a beating. In fact, my father said, a beating like the one Henry had just taken—nothing more than a few scrapes and bruises, nothing broken—was a good thing for a boy. It sharpened the teeth. When Henry didn't respond to this, our father told him to buck up.

"Damnit Henry, this is only the beginning of the fight for you! You think everything will come easy? You can't let one beating knock you down. You have to get back out there. People are counting on you."

Our mother had a very different idea of what should be done about it: they would call Sheriff Chuck Sheldon and have the two boys arrested. She knew who they were, she said. "Those two hoodlums who drive around in that red car." And then they would call Jerry MacDonnell, the district attorney, and press charges. When my father came out of the bedroom, pale and shaken, my mother rushed in and shut the door. No one but Henry knows what she said to him, for she wouldn't tell us, but she never mentioned calling Chuck again. She wouldn't even let the subject of what had happened cross our lips, and just as she predicted, Henry came down to breakfast the next morning dressed for school. He did not, however, get back out there, as our father had told him to. He left for school early to avoid walking with me and first thing broke up with Michele and quit all his activities and sports.

That night our father lost control of himself in a way I had never seen before, screaming in Henry's face that he didn't even recognize his own son. He threw a tantrum, sweeping a whole shelf of books out of the bookcase and kicking them into the fire while we all stood there watching. Finally, he leaned against the mantle, his back heaving. I could see from under his armpit that his nose was dripping like a child's, and I felt sorry for him, more sorry than I felt for Henry, who sat on the couch with a blank expression frozen on his face. Our mother squeezed her hands together.

"It's going to work out," she said. "We need to look forward."

"I don't understand!" our father said, pleading.

Michele came to the house and tried to get Henry to speak to her; the coach stopped by, along with a number of Henry's friends. Henry stayed in his room reading books he had borrowed from our father's shelf, books on war, though not for school, my parents soon discovered: he would drop from being second in the class to below the top 20 percent—the cutoff point, the guidance counselor said, for out-of-state colleges.

After he came home from serving overseas, Henry stopped speaking to our parents, who blamed it on some kind of shell shock, as my mother called it, though they both knew Henry hadn't seen any combat. He and his unit had patrolled a fence in Korea.

In the ten years after the army, he would call me, somehow finding me wherever I was at the time, from wherever he was at the time—Boulder, Denver, San Jose—and tell me about the latest place he had just traveled to. He had a long list of places he wanted to visit, he said. I never found out what he did for a living, but he seemed to have money for travel. He lived in a silver Airstream. He sent me a picture of it. He never had any plans, except where he wanted to travel next. I had worked in construction since high school, moving every couple years. I never knew where to call to give him my new number, but he always phoned every year right before I headed home for Christmas.

All morning and afternoon we waited at the house while boats and divers searched the lake for Henry. Each time the phone rang, and it seemed to ring every few minutes, we all jumped and my cousin answered, saying no, we didn't have any news. The rest of the family waited over at my aunt's house on Second Street. Even those people in town not invited to the boat party were like family to my parents, and each one of them called to express their concern. My mother offered to make us sandwiches and soup. My father asked her repeatedly to sit down, but she said we had to eat. Finally, he begged her, his voice trembling in the small square living room of the old colonial, and she shivered in place with her hands clutched in front of her stomach. She looked older to me than I had ever thought she would.

Sometime in the late afternoon Michele, Henry's high school girlfriend, called.

"Is this important?" my cousin asked before handing me the phone.

"Who was that? Was that your cousin John?" she asked. I grunted and looked his way. "Listen, Paul, you better come. Don't say anything to your parents; just come over." Her accent had thickened while mine had all but faded in the far-flung places I had lived.

I told my parents I was going out for some air. Michele had directed me up to Central Street where, in my absence, a few new houses had been built over the ridge toward the farmland. Doug Parris, who I hadn't seen since high school, met me at the door. An excellent outfielder in my brother's year, he had also been kind of a goon, at least on the outside. Despite his size, he now seemed shy. He mumbled for me to come in while looking at his feet. I noticed a Nason's Heating and Cooling van in the driveway and guessed that was what he did for a living. A child cried from the back room as Michele appeared.

"Your brother's in the rec room in the basement," Michele said, standing with both hands pressed into her hips. I leapt toward the door halfway down the hallway. "Wait a minute," she said and sat down on the couch. "He showed up here soaking wet late last night and we put him to sleep on the couch."

"What did he say?"

"He asked for you," Michele said. "But he wanted me to talk to you first. I guess that's not what he said exactly, but that's what he wants."

"I'm just happy he's here."

"Your mother came to see me five years ago. She had never said more than hello to me in the aisle at Boyton's for all those years since Henry and I broke up, then she knocks on my door and asks if we can talk about what happened. Remember those two guys who went after your brother—Rod and Denny, lived out the Chelsea Road? They didn't just beat your brother up. There was more to it. I guess she was the only one Henry told. I don't know why she decided I needed to know. Then last night he shows up dripping wet saying he had to talk to me. He kept apologizing to me as if it had all just happened, curled up on the floor down in the rec room. Rod and Denny. I'm sure they hardly knew what they'd done even after they'd done it. One of them still lives here, works down at the garage. He's married and has kids."

Downstairs, Henry hunched on the couch in a bathrobe that hung past his wrists and ankles. I sat down in the recliner opposite him. His shoulders bony, his cheeks sunken, and his skin the color of cement, he didn't look like my brother.

"Mishy talk to you?" he said.

"Henry, it doesn't make any difference."

"That's what Ma said years ago."

Lines traced down into his beard. He was losing his hair in two tracks extending along his temples and his skin there was as flushed and tender as it had been when we were young. It came as no surprise to me that I had not realized what Henry had been through. I saw no more than I had to. People were always surprising me.

"What else did Mom say to you in that room?" I asked.

I knew what she had said, though, and his silence confirmed it. She judged that Henry had a better chance of carrying the weight of what had happened on his own than our father did of surviving the shame.

"You come back here every year, don't you?" he said.

"Twice a year." These visits to our parents had been the only consistent thing in my life.

"Last night—I thought that door on the boat led to a deck. I was just going out for some air," he said, smiling and shaking his head. "I thought this might be the right time to come around. The parents wouldn't recognize anything about me anyway."

"Sure they would."

"Look," he said, "I wanted to let you know I was all right. But I also want you to do something for me. I don't want you to tell them you saw me. Mishy agreed. You don't have to lie for me. You just have to keep quiet."

"I saw them follow you into the woods," I said.

He shook his head.

"I thought they might push you around," I said, "but I—"

"No," Henry said. "No."

I pictured how our mother would react when it became clear they wouldn't find the body. Over the last ten years she had been wearing down. I asked Henry if he couldn't just forgive them, our parents. I begged him to.

"It has nothing to do with that," he said, and I nodded. I thought I knew what he meant. I, too, had grown into a person I didn't know or even like very much, and it was far too late to blame or forgive anyone for that.

"Just let them forget about me," he said. "It's the best thing for everyone."

On the way to the bus station in Augusta, he leaned down low in the passenger seat, his face tense until he found the country station on the radio. The farther upriver we drove, the more he relaxed. By the time we pulled into the terminal, he was tapping on the dash and pointing out where I should park. I realized he had been through here a few times in the last ten years, maybe even walking right by our parents' house, as he decided whether to come back or disappear forever.

He grabbed for the handle, and I asked if he couldn't just come home anyway—just put it all aside. "For her," I said, "for Ma. Think about what this will do to her."

"What makes you think she wants to see me like this?" he said. "She doesn't want to know who I am now. Neither of them do."

I hesitated long enough for him to nod and take off. After several minutes sitting frozen in the car, I ran out and found him in line for the bus. I didn't know what to say, though. I couldn't be sure that he wasn't right. He must have known what I was thinking because he smiled in the way he once had.

"You can't leave," I said.

"I already did," he said, and boarded the bus.

He was right, he had left, when he was seventeen, and I hadn't known what to do since then. I loved my brother, and he was being swept away from me again. I watched his bus descend the hill, and I wanted to think that everything would have been different if I had only followed my first instinct years before, the better part of myself, and sped through the woods to warn him about Rod and Denny. But despite what our father had always said about General Wolfe, I didn't believe that a single event could determine the course of our lives. It seemed more likely that we were swept up in the momentum of currents that reached back farther than we could see.

A message at the house said they had all gone over to the lake, and when I arrived at the shore the beach was nearly full: Chuck Sheldon, the Sheriff; all my uncles, aunts, and cousins; and all the people who had been at my father's party, crowded the dock. People Henry had known in school lined up along the shore with many of the local schoolteachers. The police boats landed and dragged their equipment up the beach.

I stared at my mother's back, wrapped tightly in her gray cardigan. She had underestimated our father years before, and now, no doubt, Henry was underestimating her, but we had all been wrong about each other for so long that I was afraid of what the truth would do to us.

The sun lowering into the trees on the opposite shore shot a fan of orange light out over the lake, turning the surface a deep purple. A few moments later the sun blinked below the horizon, and the lake fell under the shadow of the trees. I don't think any of us had expected it to end like this, my father's career and my brother's life. They had to end, though, everyone knew that, and I think a few of us felt relieved it was over.

My mother held her arms folded, her elbows gripped in her palms. When she saw me, she stared until I was sure she could read what I was trying to keep from her. Her eyes dimmed, and she came forward to wrap her arms around me.

"Oh Paul, I thought he was finally coming back to us," she said as she leaned unsteadily on my shoulder, and I said nothing.

My mother and I walked down the slope to where my father stood on the beach with his hands hanging open at his sides and his chin on his chest. The three of us joined the others looking out through the slate-gray haze. No one spoke, and not a breath stirred the smooth surface of the water.

THE LAKE

A hockey game started near shore, mostly fathers and sons and brothers in plaid jackets and blue caps, choosing sides according to size. Two boys set rocks two feet apart as a goal. It had rained and frozen over, the end of the season, and the ice was smooth.

One man raised his heavy arms and skated backward with his eyes closed, drifting out and around a rocky point where kids in the summer used a rope swing. He opened his eyes as he turned in a circle, watching the lake come into view, the gray sky above, and finally the pine forest. The chirps and scrapes of the hockey game drifted from around the corner as he skated farther out and saw a girl sitting with her stockinged knees pulled up and her mittens hoarded in her lap—Jacob Small's youngest, Katie, watching him skate. The crisp air all but swallowed a cheer—someone's goal—before it reached this skater who had just headed north when with an abrupt vanishing the ice gave way.

Underwater, his body convulsed. He thrashed once, but his gloved fist only grazed the ice before his limbs grew sluggish. He extended his hand, palm up, as he did every day at the store where he worked, waiting for the customer's money, and he saw where the ice thinned along a crack leading to the hole where he had fallen through. But it was too late for this kind of clarity. The ice, a luminous gray cap, pressed down, and he pictured Jacob Small's daughter, her small eyes watching the hole in the ice where he had vanished. He knew she would not come to the edge and reach into the water; she would not be able to without falling in herself. She ran errands to the store for her mother every other day, paying him for milk and bread, saying thank you. Otherwise he had known her only as a girl waiting for the bus with the rest, maybe standing slightly apart.

Katie Small could not stand up. For a few moments it was as if she were under water. She sat holding her breath and staring at the hole where Franklin Crawford had suddenly disappeared. She stood, ready to yell, but no one was close enough to hear her. Her new black boots crunched over the old path, breaking through the thin crust and snapping branches beneath before she was on the icy trail again slipping down the gentle slope toward the field behind the McKinley's house, where tufts of hay stood shoulder-high out of the snow. She was only a hundred yards from the hockey game, but they couldn't see around the point.

Dennis, her brother's friend, stood in the McKinley's driveway to the side of the barn kicking at something on the ground. He looked up when Katie came into view and looked right at her as he rarely did at anyone, even the girls in his own class, two years above Katie. She stopped running without realizing she had and stared at him. She rarely spoke to him when he came over to the house to see her brother. Dennis started running toward her over the thick snow of the field, raising his knees high in the air. In moments he stood beside her, brushing his pants.

"Why aren't you down playing hockey?" she asked.

"I don't know," he said and stomped his heel into the packed trail. At night kids Dennis's age, Dennis himself, came down this trail to drink beer in the woods. In the steam of Dennis's breath, at the sight of his red palms fumbling with a handful of snow, she had forgotten Franklin.

"I gotta go," Dennis said and ran off toward the lake, leaving her alone. Her legs wouldn't move. She saw the boys on the lake weaving in circles chasing a black dot. Mothers stood by a coffee thermos someone had brought down to the edge. Katie slipped once on the snow bank next to the road. Her mother and father were nowhere in sight; she saw her brother Jamie, out on the ice, his cheeks red and mouth gaping open, a look of abandoned excitement in his eyes as he prepared to defend the goal. Mrs. Johnson was the first person she reached. Katie pulled on her arm, but Mrs. Johnson was yelling to her son out on the ice to put his hat back on.

"Just a minute, hon," she said to Katie and screeched at her son again, who paid no attention.

A voice on the other side of the game rose above all the noise. "Someone has gone under the ice. Someone has gone under!" Everyone fled for shore and stumbled around in the snow on their skates as if suddenly crippled at the knees. Parents groped through the crowd for their children while a few of the men began running for their trucks and some rope. Mrs. Johnson left to find her other son while Katie stood still until her mother grabbed her arm and shook her.

"You scared me!" her mother shouted, eyes darting around as if the lake might reach out and steal Katie from the shore.

Someone shouted Franklin's name.

"Franklin Crawford," Katie's mother said. "He lived in an apartment above Dawson's."

Katie's father seemed to know no better. He read aloud from the *Crier*, nodding his head at what they all knew. Katie sat at the table counting the crackers she had not used in her soup as her mother opened the door to the stove. Inside, a pile of orange coals the size of eyeballs glowed brighter as cool air from the kitchen rushed in. Katie pictured Franklin on the bottom of the lake, his body green and gray, half rotten, jaw hanging by loose threads, dark empty sockets reflecting the world to which his soul had traveled.

Franklin's aunt told the reporter from the *Crier* that she thought he had a few friends other than the townspeople and those who lived around the lake. Yet no one in town seemed willing to come forward and admit to being his friend. She said he often went off on benders in other states where no one knew him at all. It was true he once spent six months in a county jail in New York state on charges of assault. This was news to people. He had never shown signs of this potential for deceit and violence in their village. People had always assumed Franklin was slotted to inherit his aunt's house and money, though she claimed never to have intended this at all. In fact, she told the reporter, she planned to live another sixty years, at least, and by then there would be nothing left of her money or her house. She would be one hundred and thirty.

There was no sign of the body all winter. When the ice melted, state people appeared with outboard boats and divers—a big commotion—but they found nothing.

"Surely they will find him," Mrs. Small said one morning.

Mr. Small didn't stop reading the paper. "If they dredged for him and didn't find anything, he's not down there. He probably went down river. There's a strong current down there."

"He could be caught on something at the bottom." Her mother spoke idly, as if about one of her crossword puzzles.

Her father added, "I don't want you children swimming in there until this business is over." None of the children were present, however, except for Katie.

It only rained a couple times all spring. When the air grew warm in early June, kids collected by the rope swing after school, though not as many jumped because the water was low. Mostly the boys jumped. They claimed to know where the rocks were.

Dennis backed up with the rope in his hand, swinging out and up, rising and turning straight into the air. He waved as he came around to face the shore, and for a moment Katie felt her eyes lock with his before he pointed his toes and sliced into the water. The other kids on the shore paid no attention, but Katie stared at the small patch of swirling bubbles marking the spot where Dennis had gone under. She had stepped forward enough to be noticed by two girls, who stopped talking and glared at the intruder. This was the older crowd. With a crash, Dennis's arm rose out of the water followed by his head.

"Franklin's got my leg!" he screamed and went back under. The girls to Katie's right chuckled, the one leaning back in her bikini and running a red-nailed finger over the tiny hairs leading up to her belly button.

This time Dennis waved both arms in the air.

"He's dragging me under! Someone help!"

Dennis swam under water to the edge and sprang out, his smooth, narrow chest glistening as he sauntered over the roots and pine needles to sit next to the two girls. He looked right through Katie as if she wasn't there; if he had looked again she would have been gone.

She sat down in the same spot where she had seen Franklin. She was the last one to see him alive; no one knew this. How much time had passed, she wondered, between when she saw him go under and when she reached Mrs. Johnson? Ten minutes? She had moved so slowly, as if walking to school, or to take in the laundry, or waist-deep through water at the beach in the summer. It felt as if she were still moving this slowly, still arriving too late.

Dennis came over, as he did almost every day after school, and stomped upstairs to the third floor to see her brother. After Katie finished helping her mother with chores, she went up to her room to write a letter to her friend, Julie. For six months now Katie had been sad about her best friend moving away with her parents to Vermont. Katie had asked her mother if she would drive her to Julie's new house, but her mother was too busy. So was Julie's mother. Katie had been writing every afternoon since Julie left, but Julie's letters had trickled down to every three weeks. Katie didn't care; she would write Julie if Julie didn't write back at all.

She wrote her about what she was thinking and about what people were doing around the lake. According to Julie's last letter, however, Katie didn't like people very much. Katie was currently thinking about what she would say. She couldn't remember exactly what she had said in many of the previous letters. Julie had them now. Katie loved those letters so much she wanted them back. It made her sad, thinking of them out there in the state of Vermont. They weren't hers anymore. She almost wanted them back more than she wanted Julie back. Julie seemed to know this.

In this day's letter she admitted to Julie she was maybe not so interested in people. She was thinking about what she had seen happen to Franklin. She could not remember feeling anything when Franklin disappeared. She wanted to tell someone what she had seen now almost as badly as she had the afternoon she saw it happen, which was so long ago it seemed as if she had imagined the whole thing. She was afraid, she realized, that someone would find out she had been the first one to see him go under and that she could have run faster along the path, that she had stopped when she saw Dennis—this boy she saw almost every day, who was unremarkable (Julie agreed) in all ways. Then people would know what she was really like. Sometimes when she closed her eyes, she wrote, she was afraid everyone would vanish, even Julie, and she would be alone next to the lake where her grandparents and great grandparents had lived. Julie had said before she left that Katie should not think too much before she wrote and never rewrite anything. If she just wrote down what she was thinking as it came out, then it would be as if they were still together talking. Maybe so. The letters seemed to create the shadow of a parallel life. She wondered, though, if Julie would stop reading her letters, if she would just start stacking them in a box.

The warm sun made her feel like one of the summer people who walked by the shore with ice cream dripping down their wrists. No one talked of Franklin any more; it was as if he had never existed. This was a relief but also strange, as if she expected to see him appear around the corner at school or from behind a sheet on the clothesline. He was still there, she felt, watching how she took every step and breath for granted, as if she deserved this life.

After helping her mother, she walked down to the public landing. Young kids ran up to their knees in the lake and stopped as thunder crashed. It was sunny, but a storm was coming. Mothers of the kids looked up as gray clouds inching across the sky flowed into the valley. The sailboats out on the lake lost the wind. The sailors sat upright, not speaking, staring across the glassy surface, the sails flopping lazily back and forth. Katie stayed even after the mothers packed up the kids and took them home.

Thunderheads rolled up over the hay fields and burst out into the open blue sky above the lake. Within minutes, rain sheeted across the water, moving in a line toward her with the wind, which brushed through the oak and birch and pine. Lightning streaked to some point on the far shore, followed by an echoing boom traveling down the valley. Katie ran from the beach to the porch of her house as rivers formed along the roadside and rushed down toward the lakefront. The sky had emptied a bucket, and then it stopped. She stood on the porch and looked through the rising steam at the clearing sky where a faint mist appeared before the blue, and the light shimmered off the still-soaked oak leaves and grass, creating spots in her vision when she looked away.

Dennis stayed the night. The music thumped above in her brother's room until their mother made them turn it off at eleven. Later, Katie heard her brother's feet creaking down the stairs to the kitchen and back up again. Katie slept with just a sheet and her underwear it was so hot, and even though the window was open, no breeze came in off the lake. With the sheet pulled off, the air didn't move against her skin. On a night like this it would be almost dawn before the lake cooled the air, and until then sweat glistened her face and neck and finally, late, a breeze did lift the curtains, the center of the white drapes rising into potbellies. As her bedroom door pulled open, the bellies rose up and lost their balance. The cool air pricked her skin and lips, and there stood Dennis in his white T-shirt, skinny arms dangling and jaw loose. She closed her eyes and held them closed against the urge to see what he would do before he did it. At school she saw him strutting in the hall as if he weighed two hundred pounds. He stood above her now, the electricity of his eyes raising tiny hairs on her arms and neck. He worked for his father, a carpenter, during the summer and some week-ends, and even from across the room she could feel the calluses on his hands and the way his lower lip pro-truded when his mouth hung open, most of the time, and the way his eyes, set close together, always seemed surprised and afraid of being reprimanded. Yet he stood across the room moving an inch at a time over the two-hundred-year-old pine boards, trying not to wake her. The square-head nails creaked as the breeze brushed over her skin, over her hips and eyelashes. Without warning (she had imagined him approaching forever, never arriving) he was there, breathing unsteadily, his hands poised just above her stomach like heavy air. He rested them lightly over her stomach and ribs. She opened her eyes a crack and saw him kneel-ing over her with his eyes closed and head bent, like her mother waiting for the sacrament on Sundays, only his hands were turned down.

He left quickly. By the time she looked around, there was no sign of him. His footsteps were less care-ful in their retreat, shuffling across the floor overhead.

The weight of his body pressed into the springs of the bed in her brother's room.

In the morning she lay on top of the covers until she heard her mother and father downstairs. Her two oldest brothers drove off and finally Dennis and Jamie trundled down the steps. The screen door slammed behind them. Rising, she felt heavy, her head pressed in. Her mother was too busy at the sink to turn around; her father was doing inventory at the store. The boys sat down on the porch railing, facing each other, and Dennis swung his legs.

"It takes an hour?" her brother said, continuing some conversation, but Dennis didn't answer. He pulled on his lip with his teeth, as if thinking about it, and Katie knew both what they were talking about and the answer to the question. It took a half hour to drive to Vaughn on the other side of the lake. But they had no car.

"Hey," Dennis said, suddenly speaking to her. She just stared back.

Dennis swung his legs to the other side of the railing, stood on the edge, and leapt off. He was gone. Her brother waved before turning on her.

"What are you doing here?"

"It's my house, too."

He seemed resigned, staring at the porch floor. Every boy his age was obsessed with getting around the lake to Vaughn. She didn't understand why. She had been there, as they all had, in the car with their mother.

There were more people there, more cars, a row of stores.

She turned and went back inside to the kitchen. Her mother said she was a difficult person. She went to the downstairs bathroom and looked in the mirror for outward signs of this trait, and there saw two white globes in her head, and within the white, two green circles, and at their center black dots, clear as pools of oil, reflecting her round face and wide nose.

"Mom," she said loud enough for him to hear. "Jamie is planning to walk to Vaughn."

"Good luck."

Katie sat down at the table.

"Some day," her mother said, arriving at the table with a box of cereal and a bowl but no milk, "you'll be asking me to take you there."

"No."

"Wait and see."

The train whistled two miles away. In the summer it passed slowly.

Katie helped her mother hang sheets behind the house. It didn't take long before they were done, and her mother went back inside, and Katie walked across the road to the town dock where she sat with her legs dangling in the water. Dennis appeared and walked with both hands in his pockets, hips swaying, down to the edge of the lake where he picked up a stone, looked at it for a moment, and tossed it medium distance into the water. He picked up another, larger one, and turned it over in his palm before tossing it farther out. The splash threw a small cape of water. He stood with one hip cocked, hands in his pockets again, watching the ripples spread.

When he bent over to squat, his sunburned skin pulled tight around his spine and wiry back muscles. He didn't say anything but just looked out across the lake in the general direction of Vaughn.

"I'm gonna hop that train," he said.

"To Vaughn?"

"Nah. It goes farther than that. It goes across the whole country."

She pictured long flat stretches of plains with boxcars inching across, her legs dangling out of the open doorway, swinging in turn to the click-click of the wheels against the track. How long would that take, she wondered? No water in sight. Nothing to drink. Her mouth was dry from the thought.

"I don't know why you want to go," she said.

He said she should come out with him in his brother's canoe to see the airplane at the bottom of the lake, if she hadn't seen it before, and she hadn't. She'd heard about it, as everyone had. Her mother said there was no such thing at the bottom of the lake, but the story was that thirty years before a seaplane had crashed into the lake and killed all four people aboard.

They found his brother's canoe hidden in the bushes over by the rope swing. The lake, Dennis explained, was low enough this year so they could see the plane on the bottom. He had seen it himself, just the day before, with his brother.

He pushed them off in the aluminum canoe, and after twenty minutes, he moved sideways in his seat, the paddle across his knees, the skin around his stomach in fine tight folds. He closed his eyes and shrugged one shoulder as water slowly dripped off the blade of the paddle. She couldn't tell if they were there or if he was taking a rest.

"During the week you work for your father?" she said.

"Yep."

She pictured him stacking boards and cleaning up scrap lumber from early in the morning until dinner.

"I'm supposed to be helping him today."

"Why aren't you?"

"Didn't feel like it."

"Isn't he going to be mad?"

"Guess so."

"What are you going to tell him?"

"Nothing. I'm not going to tell him nothing."

"So where's the airplane?"

"We're right on top of it. Go ahead. Look down."
He was trying not to be proud of himself.

She didn't want to look down. She didn't expect it to be here, right under them.

"Go ahead, look down," he said again, and she did because she didn't want him to think she was scared.

There was nothing beneath the flat surface but green, and flecks in the green, drifting in the sunlight.

"Don't you see it?"

Just as he said this she did see an outline, possibly a wing. When she looked harder there may also have been something attached to the wing, and she looked away quickly.

When the canoe drifted out of the sunlight, she saw the full shape of the plane, pale against the dark mud and algae of the bottom. Dennis stood up and dove into the water, his legs kicking down until she had to look away her heart pounded so fast. For a moment she was outside her body, above the lake looking down at herself, a girl she didn't know, sitting alone in a canoe. There were other people on the lake, but in her mind she was looking at a girl in a canoe alone on a lake. It had never seemed odd before to live next to such a large body of water, like a glassy eye peering up out of the earth.

"Almost made it." He breathed frantically, water spurting out of his mouth and his eyes bulging slightly out of their sockets, as if they were starved for air. His neck stretched, his mouth widening, and he was under again, his long pale limbs pushing against the water like the slow glide of a great blue heron landing on the lake in the hazy dusk. Then she could no longer distinguish his body from the body of the plane. He rose, eyes closed, arms at his sides and legs kicking. His face was blissful and beautiful, as if in sleep. His arms burst over the gunwale, tilting the canoe so Katie had to lean the other way.

"I saw the cockpit." He wheezed and coughed, gulping for air. "I saw into the cockpit. Nothing was there. Do you wanna come down and see?"

She shook her head.

"I didn't bring my bathing suit."

He looked off toward the beach. Maybe someone was there. Someone he'd rather be with. She wasn't about to look. It didn't matter. He might as well go over there.

"How you going to get back in the canoe?"

He shrugged and kept looking across the lake.

"You sure you don't want to come in?"

"I don't have my suit."

He seemed not to hear.

"How you going to get up?"

"Easy."

"It doesn't look easy to me. You'll tip the canoe over."

He pushed off, watching her as he sank back into the water: first his shoulders, then his neck and the back of his head, his chin and finally his eyes, still open, sinking. He was gone. She could not see the blurry outline of his body beneath the water. Without warning, he rose over the high stern and pressed down, the muscles in his arms bulging. He tumbled over the seat and collapsed sideways on the bottom with his rib cage expanding and contracting, the water rolling off his skin.

For a moment he seemed to stop breathing and hold absolutely still.

She leaned over to touch the knob of his shoulder. It was colder than she expected, like the hard edge of an underwater rock. He lay with the side of his head pressed against the bottom of the canoe.

"I can hear the lake humming," he said.

He sat up abruptly and gazed off in the direction of Vaughn.

"I'm planning on getting outta here," he said.

"You mean to Vaughn?"

"No. I already been there. I'm gonna keep going."

"Where?"

"Don't know yet."

Dennis hardened his jaw and flexed his toes.

"You going to jump the train?"

He nodded.

But she knew he wasn't going anywhere. He would just talk about it, like her brothers.

She woke before sunrise and sat up in bed. The train whistle had woken her, though she hadn't heard it. Now she could hear the faint rumble in the distance of the train passing out of town. She sat in her room at her desk with a pen poised above paper, trying to think of what to write Julie. For the first time, she had nothing to say. She felt empty, like skin filled with water.

Dear Julie,

I have decided to leave this place. If you receive no more letters from me for a long time it is because I am no longer here.

I promise to look for you in the future, in Vermont or wherever you are.

There is no need to write back your promise. Whenever you get this letter, and read it, just say, "I promise."

She thought for a minute more.

We promised before you left to always tell each other the truth. You are the only one I have ever promised that to. Last time I wrote that maybe I didn't like people, but it's not true that I don't like you. I love you. Just like we said to each other before you left. But the reason I have to leave here is that a man is dead. I didn't mean it at all.

She collected some clothes in her backpack and waited for her mother to step out of the kitchen, then walked out the front door and down the steps. Her brother Jamie and her oldest brother were down by the lake. Her oldest brother stood apart, not wanting to be too close to the younger one, and she passed to the right, into the woods, to avoid being seen by any of them. Her mother stood behind the house next to the clothesline. For a moment she expected to be caught, but her mother stared out to the edge of the woods, at the fringe of darkness, with one hand resting on the pole of the clothesline, as she crossed the McKinley's field to the lake trail.

When the shore grew rocky and steep, she turned inland into the woods, uphill over sudden oval hollows where trees had been uprooted so long ago that they had rotted into the earth, their sprawling roots hanging in the air. She was led forward by the patches of light filtering through the canopy of oak leaves and floating in curtains of dust and pollen, the air itself surprised, caught in the act of holding the light. She headed down a slope to the narrow trickle of a stream and ran up the opposite slope, listening to the dry branches snap beneath her heels, the thud of her pack against her shoulders.

Her breath steamed into the air, bats flitted like dark hands, and her shoes clicked against the pebbles of a streambed. She followed the stream, having no more energy to climb. Everything was still except for the water trickling over and around a trail of stones. Maybe she had been on a long trip. Her legs felt that way, and that's what she would say if she met anyone who didn't want to rape or kill her but just wanted a conversation. She stopped walking and held her hand out in the air. She felt the train at the edge of town, pushing through the woods along its cleared path.

The ground flattened and the stream submerged in the soft earth. Dead, dried out pines sent her around to the right where she had to push forward through a tangle of bushes to reach a clearing. The heat of the afternoon sun collected here, thickening the damp air. Fallen branches hung above her in the branches of other trees, several of which stood only by leaning against their living neighbors.

There was no easy way forward through the tangles, but she wanted to see the lake once more before she reached the train and left forever. She closed her eyes and saw what she would see when she reached the lake: flashing lights and trucks, the people of her town gathered down by the water's edge. Her mother would run back and forth in front of the house yelling her name while her brothers checked the beach and still others, assuming the worst, took to boats with the same grappling hooks they had used to drag for Franklin. They would comb the bottom for her body but never find it.

The sweat rolled down her face. She could see Franklin's face, ruddy and unshaven, his jaw hanging open as he skated over the smooth ice. He was there, and then he wasn't. It seemed that it had all started with her, as if the earth had opened beneath Franklin in response to her own indifference.

She reached the lake's edge and looked across the flat water and saw her house and the pebbled shore of the town landing. They reminded her of nothing she had known. The tiny figures moving lazily along the shore might be her brothers, but she couldn't tell. Cars passed along the shore road. One parked at the landing, and someone got out. It seemed like a place anyone might live, not the place where she had lived, and there were no signs of a search for her.

Of course they knew. It was impossible not to know in their house, in their town, when someone was missing, even for a day. They knew, they just weren't doing anything about it. Maybe she had already been explained away.

None of the people of her town or her family were who they thought they were. Even if she, Katie, vanished under the surface, her mother and all the rest would cry for a while and mope, especially walking downtown, but in the end they would feel a secret relief that it wasn't them. If she went back, she was not going to say anything about it, not for the rest of her life.

Tonight the dinner table would be full except for her place. Twenty years from now she would return, come up to her mother while she hung clothes on the line in back of the house, and rest a hand on her back. Her mother would have gray hair and dim eyes and thin hands like Katie's grandmother's. But there would be nothing to say when she returned, and she would return right now; she had to—she was from here. The images of all that she had seen would be erased when she was buried in the plot behind the Methodist church on the hill above the lake.

She followed the shore and arrived in less than an hour to stand at the edge of the woods by the McKinley's field looking across the rock beach near her house. Dennis stood by the water kicking at something with the toe of his boot. He was dressed in his work clothes and had probably just finished working for his father. Maybe he thought she would never come home, that she had drowned, and this was all he could think to do. To see that nothing would change if she died was to know that she had never lived. She wanted to call out to him, to hear his voice return, but something in her resisted and watched for him to raise his chin so she could see her absence on his face. A wave of heat passed up her body and washed through her eyes as she waited for him to realize she was there. He turned around and looked up, as if at a mountain peak or a descending plane, but there was nothing above except a line of high white clouds pulling up over the valley like a cold sheet.

WHY THE DEVIL CHOSE
NEW ENGLAND FOR HIS WORK

At the far end of the pond a beaver slapped its tail. Andrew had seen it there earlier in the summer, its brown head cutting across the glassy surface. The McNeils, alone on the other side of the beach with their two young kids, stood up and shielded their eyes to see, but Andrew's mother didn't stir from where she lay on the towel with her chin raised and her palms open to the sky.

Out on the float in the middle of the pond a kid in denim shorts, Andrew's age or maybe older, walked to the edge of the diving board and bounced lightly with his toes curling off the edge and his arms hanging loosely at his sides. Andrew hadn't seen him either walking down the beach or swimming. The kid stared at something in the water as he bounced, higher each time, and Andrew waited for him to dive off, but he didn't. He stopped bouncing, stood still for a moment on the end of the board, and finally backed up. A gust shivered across the surface of the water, which caught the angle of the light, and Andrew's eyes stung from the glare and he had to look away. There was a splash, and when he looked again the float was empty. The kid appeared on the beach with his black hair dangling over his nose and his pale tight shoulders knotted like roots. He held a turtle in his hands.

The kid wandered around a bend in the shoreline, and Andrew followed, walking along the beach. The kid stood in a small cove where the sand turned to mud. Andrew stopped twenty feet away and watched the turtle's head stretch across the mud, mouth gaping.

"Hey," the kid said, and Andrew nodded. The whistle of the Boston-Maine lowed from the edge of town. "I know who you are," the kid said, half under his breath, as if talking to himself. "I heard about your sister drowning a couple months back."

"How'd you know about that?" Andrew said.

"I've been living over in Monmouth with my grandma, but I'm from here. I just moved back. You know my little sister Tiny Small?"

Andrew said he did.

"Everybody does," the kid said and stood up, holding a stone between his fingers. Andrew was sure he would aim at the turtle, which slowly pushed its way toward the water, but he just held the stone in the air and then rolled it into his palm.

"Andrew!" His mother called from around the corner, and after a second she called again. The sound of
her voice slid across the water and disappeared.

"That's you, right?" the kid said. He knelt down,
picked the turtle up, and rested it on the surface of the
pond. The shell floated for a moment and sank.

Andrew's mother called again and again, but he
didn't move until he could hear something in the timber of her voice that he had heard the last time she had
yelled his sister's name.

"I have to go now," Andrew said, and the kid nodded.

Today was Old Vaughn Day, and the town, founded
just after the Revolution, was celebrating its two hun-
dredth anniversary this July with the Whatever Race
down the river and a parade on Water Street. Andrew's
father was in the lawn mower brigade, a group of guys
from the Vaughn softball team who dressed up every
year to push lawn mowers down Water Street. From
the kitchen window, Andrew could see the last few
rafts of the race struggling downriver, manned by the
new friends his father had made since Stephanie's
death: women in braids and flowered skirts, men with
long hair. Andrew agreed with his mother that they
smelled, and not just of sweat. Drugs, hemp, compost.
In the last five years, they had come from all over and
moved to the woods on the edge of town. Rubber
booters, people called them, because they went around

in rubber boots even when it wasn't raining. They made their own wine, and some of them had pottery for sale at Boyton's.

No one, not even his parents, had mentioned his sister Stephanie in over a month, even though she had only died in March. Andrew stood in the kitchen and tried to remember the last thing Stephanie had said, but he could only picture her blank face as she sat at the table eating dinner the night it happened. She had pushed her fish away half-eaten.

He moved from one window to the next, looking at the river from different angles. Out in the current a giant beer can with a man on top, drinking a beer, drifted, trailing a Volkswagen bus on pontoons. A group of bearded men in a canoe decorated as a banana latched on to one of the log breaks built in the middle of the channel.

Upstairs, Andrew asked his mother if she was going down to see the parade. She lifted her arm from in front of her face and let it fall off the side of the bed.

"Andrew, listen to me for a minute," she said. "I don't want you hanging around that kid from the pond. He's one of the Smalls. All right?" Andrew nodded and she turned away from him onto her side. "Now, go on down to the parade. I'll be along in a while." She stretched her toes. He knew she wouldn't go. When she wasn't at work now, she spent most of her time napping.

The door to Stephanie's bedroom had been closed since the day of the funeral, and he was afraid to open it. The morning before she died, he had walked right in and stood above where she sat with her legs splayed, flipping through a stack of records. The way she paused to consider each one, she didn't seem to be looking for any particular album.

In the middle of her second year at the University of Southern Maine, where she had been studying physical therapy, Stephanie had taken a bus to Augusta and called from the station. Andrew had answered the phone, but without saying hello she asked for their mother, who stood a few feet away at the kitchen counter correcting student spelling tests. At dinner she didn't explain why she was home. She talked about the guy she had sat next to on the bus, and asked her parents about people they all knew in Vaughn. Afterward, Andrew heard Stephanie and their mother whispering in the laundry room. For a brief second as he crossed the kitchen to the TV room, he caught sight of Stephanie's face, her eyes closed and mouth slightly open as she leaned on the dryer. Her hair was tangled, and there were dark circles under her eyes. Something had happened to her down in Portland; she wasn't the same. Their mother, who usually chattered away when Stephanie came back from school, cinched her mouth, as if afraid something ugly would slip out.

After she came home, Stephanie wouldn't see any of her old friends. Andrew knocked several times on her door (sometimes when she was home they talked for hours into the night), but she either pretended not to be there, or told him harshly to leave her alone. At dinner every evening, no one talked. Their father asked her questions about classes, but she just gave one-word answers.

Andrew pushed open the door to her bedroom. Everything inside, the pile of clothes on the bed, the towel on the chair, even the records fanned across the carpet, remained unchanged from the morning before she died, when he had stood above her until she sighed and looked up at him. He had only wanted her to say one word, but she wouldn't. Her brown hair had loosened from the bandanna and fallen over her sweater.

Andrew walked downtown, where the fire hall committee had decorated Water Street with banners and ribbons and set up booths for raffles and hot dogs. Some of the people living above the shops had hung red, white, and blue banners or Christmas lights out of their windows. The high school band warmed up at the edge of town, and eventually the fire truck passed with the volunteer firemen sitting stolid under the sun in their full gear. The American Legion followed, gray faces held level as they marched. 4H came next: a number of girls Andrew knew from school led a cow from old man Vaughn's farm. Finally, Andrew's father and the rest of the lawn mower brigade appeared, dressed this year as Zulu warriors in grass skirts and straw hats, their faces and bellies black with shoe polish. The Vaughn High marching band, bringing up the rear, couldn't drown out the lawn mower brigade's ritualistic grunts as they pushed their mowers and pumped their fists in the air.

Andrew watched until the parade had passed and the people had followed in its wake, the dull racket dissipating farther down Water Street. Then he followed the street up the hill to the tracks. His friends Chris and Tom came out from behind the library, and he waited for them to crest the hill and disappear. After his sister died, they had stopped by once and stood in his bedroom for ten minutes looking at their shoes. When he came back to school, they kept to the other side of the lunchroom, glancing at him over their milk, never crossing over to say anything. Even teachers backed away, as if they might catch something from him. Eventually Chris and Tom started coming around again, talking about getting a softball game together, as if nothing had happened.

Andrew walked along the tracks, balancing on one of the rails with his arms out. At the edge of town the tracks passed through a tunnel of maples and came out into a field overlooking the river. The sun had slipped lower, and in the distance the musicians for the Old Vaughn Day street dance started to warm up on Water Street. The strum of an electric guitar humming along the rails reminded him of what August had once been to him: long clear afternoons sitting in the grass waiting for his mother to finish working in the garden and take them to the pond. The sun blinked below the tree line and the feeling fled just as quickly as it had arrived. The empty rail line curved into the shadows. He wanted to say Stephanie's name, but the twilight seemed made of glass, and lately his mother had been telling him when he left the house that he should be careful. "Please be careful, Andrew."

The sky darkened as he watched the river. After a while, he made his way back to the middle of town and walked along Second Street as the tinny voice of the singer for the street dance skipped over the buildings and cobblestones, coming up behind him off the face of the Methodist Church and drifting with him down the alley between Slate's Diner and Boyton's Market. They had blocked off Water Street and set up a stage overlooking the river. Most of the town was there, Andrew saw, dancing and milling about under the band's work lights. The three members of the local band—the owner of the Wharf Pub, the gym teacher, and the gym teacher's wife—strummed their guitars. People's faces passed in and out of the glare from the lights, their eyes flickering. Three kids who must have been from a nearby town, or from as far away as Augusta (he had seen them at basketball games), ducked into the alley just two feet in front of him and pulled out a bottle, which they passed between them.

"I don't see her," one of them said.

"Over there. Over there by Dom's."

They shot into the crowd, trailing the scent of stale cigarettes. It was humid, the air heavy and still above the dancers. The men up front had taken off their shirts and tied them around their waists or just let them drop to the curb as they closed their eyes and swung their arms over their heads. Many of them were friends of his father. A small, braless woman, so skinny that she might have been a twelve-year-old but for the deep creases in her sweaty face, kept lowering to her knees and rising again, as if preparing to jump off a dock. On the other side of the street, Alice Stewart raised her face to the yellow glow of the light. Her eyes were wide and blank. She had been a friend of Stephanie's and used to come over for dinner and chat with his mother about the First Baptist fund-raisers.

A dark shape appeared in the crowd, a black face with white eyes flashing in the work lights. Andrew bolted forward, calling for his father to wait, but by the time he had pushed through the sweaty bellies and armpits, his father was gone. Andrew headed toward the back of the crowd, through layers of glazed faces all turned downriver in the direction of the music, their eyes half-closed but shifting. He knew each one of them—Mr. Dawson from Dawson's Variety; Mr. Nason; Mrs. Mills, Sara Mills's mother; and Andrew's two uncles from Monmouth, both with their wives— but tonight their faces were relaxed and blissful, as if they were half-asleep. He tried to look away but couldn't; they were distant cousins of the people they were in the daylight. Not even the three-story brick buildings looked the same in the band's work lights. Shadows from lampposts lay back against empty windows.

His father bent over, heaving, near the entrance to Rexall Drugs. Andrew called to him and he whirled around. His eyes were flushed and wide, and vomit dripped from his chin. Stumbling backward, he seemed to focus briefly on Andrew's face. "Go!" he slurred. "Leave me alone!"

Andrew tripped, reeling against someone he recognized from the summer softball games, when people from the Wharf played teams from other towns. He had never seen his father drunk before. When he looked around, his father was already gone, and Andrew felt himself about to cry. He squeezed his eyes shut, but the rising din of the electric guitar made it too hard to concentrate on not crying; he thought about his mother sleeping in their unbearably quiet house.

When he opened his eyes he saw, at the back of the crowd, just inside the band lights, the kid from the pond standing with his hands in his pockets. There was a sudden break in the music, and the silence seemed to draw them closer together. He wore a blue mechanic's jacket with EDDIE written on the chest.

"Come on," the kid said and started walking away from the music. Andrew rushed to catch up. "You don't know my brother, I don't think. When he lived here, I would come over from my grandma's in Monmouth and we'd throw the Frisbee down at the landing." He stopped suddenly and looked over his shoulder in the direction of the band. The music had started up again.

"Where we going?" Andrew asked. He looked around for his father again but still didn't see him.

"To the mouth of God," Eddie said, and started running. "Hurry."

They ran along Water Street, turned up Union, and Eddie stopped where the small steel train bridge spanned high over Second Street. Eddie pulled himself up by the thick grass and crawled into a close space eroded out where the bridge met the riverbank. Andrew climbed up after him, and they sat facing each other beneath a grated metal roof that separated them from the tracks above. Eddie tossed a stone that rolled down the bank onto Second Street.

"My brother got back at six-thirty tonight," Eddie said. "Five days on the road hitching from Florida. Half a year in the pen down there." Eddie's voice quickened without rising, as if he were in a hurry to say everything before it was too late. "You know what he said when the judge sent him up? Best feeling he ever had. The one thing about my brother is he never lied, never once. How many people around here can say that?" Eddie rested his chin on his chest.

"What did he go to jail for?" Andrew asked.

"Beating this guy almost to death down in Florida. Twice his size."

"Over what?"

The ground vibrated. Andrew couldn't tell how far away the train was until all at once the air shook tears from his eyes and a metal roar rammed through his thoughts. Eddie opened his mouth, and even in the dim light, Andrew could see all the way to the back of his throat.

The train passed and the air hummed around them. Andrew felt far away, even though he was less than a mile from home.

Eddie climbed out into the night, scrambled down to the street, and started kicking pebbles. "I want you to meet my brother. I wish I could tell you what time, but I don't know. I could say noon down at the landing, but then that might not be when, either. I have to clean out the Thunderbird tonight," he said. "Tiny's been keeping chicken feed in there. He's not gonna like that. I gotta do that now. I gotta clean it out." He slouched away in the direction of the concert, leaning forward with his hands in his pockets and his head slumped. Suddenly, he stopped to look back at Andrew and run his hands through his hair. "If we're not outside your house, I guess you'll know."

The next morning Andrew looked out his bedroom window, but there was no sign of Eddie. The church bells sounded, and cars full of people passed by on their way to Sunday morning services. Usually his mother would be at the First Baptist; usually Andrew and his sister would be with her, but in June, several months after the accident, his mother had stopped going, and so had Andrew.

Downstairs, she called out that breakfast was ready, but he didn't move, and she didn't call again. He sat on his bed looking out the window. Nothing stirred for an hour, and then cars headed back up the hill and north along Second Street. Andrew went downstairs and outside to the backyard, where he saw the door was open to the shed: his father was working on stained glass. His latest idea for making money.

Andrew saw Pastor MacInnis appear on the road, walking up the hill with his shoulders square in his black jacket and his head lowered, his Bible in hand. Before the pastor looked up, Andrew rushed to open the door of the station wagon in the driveway and lay down on his back along the cool vinyl seat to hide. He listened to the pastor's leather heels crunch over last winter's sand and snap over the bricks his father had lain as a path to the door. The pastor went in through the kitchen.

Half an hour passed as Andrew stared at dead bugs caught in the dome light above his head. The heat accumulated in the car and a layer of sweat formed on his brow. He didn't want the fresh air, he didn't want to be discovered. Pastor MacInnis had been the pastor of the First Baptist Church when Andrew's mother was young, and he still was. The pastor was in there telling his mother they all had to go back—to church, to the way they were before. They couldn't, though.

Eventually, the pastor shut the door firmly and walked along the bricks. Andrew held his breath, but it was no good. The pastor stopped, turned around, and came back to the car. After a pause, he opened the door. Andrew sat up as the pastor bent down in front of him. Andrew sensed the pastor's defeat, and not just in bringing his mother back. His milky eyes passed over Andrew's face while his hand squeezed the leather Bible. It could be that his mother was right: after so many years, the pastor was tired. That's the reason she had given for not going to service anymore: the pastor was tired, and she was tired.

The pastor studied the backs of his own hands and shook his head. "How are you, son?"

Andrew said he guessed he was fine.

"It's not just herself your mother has to think of. There's you. We turn our backs on many of the things God calls evil, and pretend they don't exist, or that we don't know about them. Look what your sister did."

"What do you mean?" Andrew said. "It was an accident." He didn't know if it was, though. No one had said what it was, not to him.

The pastor smiled and shook his head. "Yes, well," he said in a much lower voice. "If the Lord could be fooled by the Devil's charm, what chance did your poor sister have against him?" The pastor reached out to squeeze Andrew's hand. "Something that appears glamorous or forbidden excites our curiosity, and we want more of it. But the people who do evil know that, and they use these things to attract those who are weak in their faith. They cannot sleep till they do evil; they are robbed of slumber till they make someone fall." The pastor let go of Andrew's hand and rose to leave. "She got caught up with the wrong people down in Portland."

Inside, his mother sat with the shades drawn and her hands folded on the kitchen table. The lamp from the next room dimly lit the side of her face.

"What did he say?" Andrew asked. She didn't stir, and in the silence a drop fell from the sink tap into a bowl of water. She was farther away now than she ever had been, farther away than her bedroom or her job or her mother's place up the hill.

"Don't you remember, we were going to cut your hair today," she said, standing suddenly and going to the drawer for the comb and scissors.

She forgot so much lately, he was surprised she remembered.

"I have to meet someone, though," he said.

"Who?" she said, setting the chair up and then dipping a comb in the sink. She looked at him. "That Small kid?"

"His name is Eddie," Andrew said.

"Didn't you hear what I said? There is something wrong with that kid—with all of them."

Andrew sealed his mouth shut. He wasn't going to answer her.

"Now that his grandma drank herself into the hospital for the last time, I guess he'll be living here in Vaughn."

"Is she dead?" Andrew asked.

She paused before answering. "She won't live. The postman found her facedown in her driveway—she was there the whole weekend. They found Eddie in the house watching TV. He didn't call anyone or do anything, just sat there."

She straightened his bangs flat. The dull edge of the scissors pressed on his forehead and with a slow grinding snip his bangs flecked into his lap. She ran her hand over his brow, smoothed the hair against the back of his neck, and rested her hand briefly on top of his head. The weight of her fingers made him tired and he closed his eyes as she continued cutting.

"There's someone at the door," she said, even though no one had knocked.

It was Eddie, Andrew knew, before he even looked out the kitchen window. His mother opened the door and Eddie came into the dark room. He stood by the counter with his hands at his sides and his lower lip clamped over his upper. He brushed the hair out of his face, but it fell back in place again.

"Please sit down," Andrew's mother said and put the comb and scissors back in the drawer, her hands fumbling.

Eddie did as he was told, burying his hands so far under the table that his back curved over his lap.

"Do you want something to drink?" she asked as she folded the dish towel.

"No, ma'am. I ate before."

His mother stiffened with her back turned, as if Eddie had cursed at her. Eddie raised his head and looked around as he tapped his heels slowly and quietly.

"My grandmother was born in this house," he said. "But I never was inside it."

Andrew's mother turned around and opened her mouth several times but couldn't get started. "My father bought the place in 1950," she finally said.

"I know," Eddie said without looking up. "He bought it from my grandpa."

"The one who owned the garage."

"Yes, ma'am," he said, and raised his face, his eyes flashing faster than a cat's tongue.

Andrew's mother stared at Eddie for a full minute. Andrew got up and moved around the kitchen, trying to get his mother to look away, and finally she did, walking into the next room where she simply stood half-turned in front of the window, her hands on her hips and her eyes opening and shutting.

"We're gonna go out for a while," Andrew called.

His mother looked at him, and he thought her eyes defied him to leave; he stared straight back at her until he couldn't stand it anymore, and then he walked out the door.

Eddie left, too, and with his head lowered he walked down the hill. Andrew followed five steps behind until they reached the landing, a green the size of a playing field, on the bank of the river where people launched their boats. There didn't seem to be anyone there. A faded green T-Bird was parked on the street. Eddie kicked a stone across the grass, and on the far side of the field the brother stood up. His eyes were copper, reflecting the light in the current of the river, and wet, as if they had been cut with a cold wind. His blond hair was parted carefully in the middle and it curled in delicate wisps. Instead of going over, Eddie stood in front of the dock and wrapped his arm around one of the tarred posts. The brother was naked above his cutoffs, and so skinny that every bone and ridge flexed as he moved. He shook his hair and pulled a yellow Frisbee from under his elbow. Without bending his body, he twisted his arm and flicked the Frisbee, which sailed across the brown backdrop of the ebb tide where seagulls picked in the mud. The Frisbee hovered and dropped gently into Andrew's hands. He didn't know if he was supposed to throw it back or hold onto it. The brother had turned away with his hands in his pockets and his elbows angled out. His pale shoulder blades twitched like nervous eyelids.

Eddie held out his hands and Andrew threw him the Frisbee, which Eddie then tossed to the brother. It was a perfect throw, soaring through the air to land in the brother's bony hands. For several minutes, the brothers continued tossing it between themselves, as if they had forgotten Andrew. The brother caught the Frisbee with one hand, turned it over, and tossed it back with the other hand. He had a way of setting the Frisbee aloft so that it lingered and spun in the liquid air.

Suddenly, the brother just sat down and leaned back. He called something to Eddie without turning away from the river, and the wind swallowed all but the flat tone of his voice. Eddie threw the Frisbee to Andrew and walked along the edge of the bank to see what his brother wanted. Andrew ran his fingers over the faded gold lettering on the rounded edge of the Frisbee and felt a warm buzzing in his head, as he did when he woke from a dream. Eddie and his brother talked about something and then crossed over to the curb. Andrew followed them and looked down at the T-Bird, with its ripped seats and sun-cracked dash.

"Get in," Eddie said, his voice a current Andrew wouldn't have been able to resist even if he had wanted to. The brother drove past town hall and turned up the hill. They pulled to a stop, idling at the corner opposite the junior high where Andrew's old friends Chris and Tom were tossing a baseball. Chris stopped his throw midway and stared at the car. Tom turned around and dropped his arms at his sides at the sight of Andrew riding low in the backseat. Then the brother hit the gas, and the long car shifted back on its haunches as they banked around the corner and sped east, out of town. Eddie tuned the radio to a country station, but even with the volume down, the speakers cracked on the low notes. Every few minutes the brother turned and spoke to Eddie, but Andrew couldn't hear a word over the wind that ripped through the open window. He held the Frisbee in his lap and watched the rush of trees pass by. The car floated over the dips and rises as they sped up, sizzling through wet spots in the road left over from that morning's rain. The air was still damp and soft above the ragged spruce tops. The road led them through hay fields that surrounded the Monmouth lakes. Andrew's whole body relaxed. He wanted the drive to go on forever, around and around the lakes, never straying too far from Vaughn but never going back.

They drove in silence around one of the lakes and returned on the same road toward town, finally pulling up in front of the Small's faded red house on a ledge above the tracks. The yard was surrounded by chicken wire, and in the corner next to the coop there was a bunch of old living room furniture. The brother sat down in a rotten recliner. Eddie planted himself on a milk crate and began pulling up grass from between his feet.

Another guy, a friend of the brother's, appeared from around the side of the house and let out a low whistle.

"I told you so," the friend said and peered down over the ledge at the tracks.

The brother rose to his feet and went over to a clothesline, passing a foot in front of Andrew without seeming to notice him. He trailed a corroded odor that he had either given to or taken from the inside of the T-Bird, and he started picking his clothes off the line; a pair of faded jeans, undershirts yellowed in the pits, a row of gray socks, which he dropped in a cardboard box. The jeans he rolled up like a towel and placed on top.

"We used to be down there for hours playing Frisbee," the brother said over his shoulder. "One of the first things I was gonna do, but when I got down there I didn't wanna be there."

The brother's friend nodded without turning away from the tracks.

"So you're the kid whose sister went into the river last March," the brother said. It took Andrew a minute to realize the brother was talking to him.

"I was in when it happened, but my brother here sent me the papers from Maine. Nothing else to do, except play basketball. I saw this girlie drowned in the river and when I saw her name I thought, shit, I know her from 'fore I went down to Florida, from that bar in Portland—that fuckin' hole on Commercial Street, the Moon What a friggin' waste, a tough one like that putting herself in the river."

"She was *tough* all right," the brother's friend said.

"It made me wish I'd been there," the brother said. "Have a few words with her. What was the name a that chump she was wet for? MacDougal's friend."

"Mirack."

The brother shrugged and looked right at Andrew. "Hey," he said. "I was thinking you could ask your father about splitting wood for him this fall. I see you got about six cord over the side of the house."

"He splits it himself," Andrew said.

"Does, huh? Well, you tell him I'm gonna split it for him this fall. Fast and cheap, you tell him."

The brother's friend sat down in one of the chairs and leaned back, laughing without sound.

The brother shook his head. "Now don't wake the dee-ceased."

There was something wrong with them, the brother and his friend. The friend shook his head with his eyes closed, a wide grin across his face. Andrew told himself he should leave, run, but he couldn't move. "She fell in," he said.

"Is that what they told you?" the brother said.

"That's what happened."

"No it ain't. That's what they told you happened. Was she walking along and fell over? No, cause in March the ice packs ten feet tall along that bank from here to Augusta down to Dresden. I know, I used to pull my uncle's icehouse before the thaw. She'd had to crawl out that drift ice and slide down on her ass to the channel."

In the dirty window of the house, an old man's face appeared but seemed not to see them. He chewed on his cracked lips until Tiny Small pushed him out of the way and pressed her forehead to the glass, with her mouth moving, talking either to the old man or to them.

The brother grabbed the friend by the arm. They headed toward the car, and both of them leaned over something the friend had in his hands.

Tiny Small appeared at Andrew's side, her nose and chin curving toward each other, her eyes scrunched like a mole's, her skin the color of paste. Her hair was like Eddie's, ink black. She had been at Andrew's school, in Special Ed, until she stopped showing up. Now she talked at him with the urgency of someone being chased, her hands held out to her sides, fingers splayed, and her words cataloged a list of desires: "I would like a Hostess Fruit Pie and a milk shake have you ever been to Portland I hope it does not rain on Saturday I want to go to Portland it does not rain there my brother Matt said I said I was I was I was I was— Andrew. Andrew," she repeated and finally closed her eyes with relief, as if all these other words had led her to the right one.

"Leave us alone, Tiny Small," Eddie said from behind his hair.

At the sound of his voice, she started again: "If I does I is going to buy me something I won't tell me what but do you think I could I could I could I could chop some wood I had a Hostess Fruit Pie this morning Mamma." She stopped again on this last word and stared at her brother.

"Yeah," Eddie said and stood up. He took Andrew's arm and pulled him away from Tiny Small. "Come on." Eddie led them down the hill, and Andrew knew they were going to his house a half mile away. Andrew wasn't sure he wanted to go there, but Eddie took them.

The door to his father's shop was still open, and when they went into the house, he saw that his mother was asleep on the couch. Upstairs, Andrew paused on the way to his bedroom. Stephanie's door was open. Eddie pushed his way inside, where, since this morning, the curtains had been stripped, the rug taken up, the books pulled off the shelves, the room made empty. Even the picture nails had been removed, leaving small black pinpricks. Eddie lay back on the wood floor and closed his eyes. Andrew sat down on the bed and looked out the window.

Across the street, a red glow appeared inside a dim upstairs room of Mrs. Shumaker's house, where a cigarette perched on her fingers. Kids in school said she had been desperate for sex after her husband left for Augusta—a woman in her forties without a husband or kids or family. The red glow flared when she inhaled a long breath. In the rhythm of the glow moving to and from her mouth, Andrew thought he recognized the echo of a pattern that he had never noticed before. He looked at the house next door and had the same feeling. Out on the rope swing, Mr. Sawyer's daughter played her game of twisting the two ropes together into a coil and then sitting on the seat to spin like a top. She spun in silence, stood in the middle of the lawn for a moment afterward like an unsteady drunk, and then did it again.

In the week before Stephanie drowned, Andrew heard her late at night walking through the house. The floorboards creaked for two beats of his heart, paused, and creaked again. Eventually, he realized she was going from window to window. On the night she drowned, the river boomed as shelves of ice along the banks crashed into the frozen river mud at low tide. He pictured Stephanie walking out the door and down the dark street to the landing by the river, her breath steaming in front of her face. The moon shone full over the neap tide, illuminating the ice flows. She scaled the jagged rubble and looked down through the thin ice where silver air pockets raced like panicked fish in the current. She knew that what was about to happen was no accident.

"Let's go," Eddie said abruptly, and leapt to his feet. He led them downstairs and out the side door, which he somehow knew how to find, and up the hill behind the house. Andrew asked where they were going, but Eddie didn't answer. After a mile or so, Andrew saw they were headed to Vaughn Stream.

At the top of the hill, Eddie said, "My brother showed me this spot. No one else knows about it except him and me." Andrew knew this wasn't the case. His father had wanted him to swim there just a few days ago—his father went there every summer, following the stream through the woods to a clearing where an old white oak towered over a deep pool. Everyone knew the guys who hayed for old man Vaughn swam in the stream at lunch. Eddie had lied, but there was nothing about his lie that made it seem untrue.

Eddie ran down the slope of the green hill toward the water and called for Andrew to hurry as he tugged his shirt over his head. He waved Andrew on and pulled the rope away from the tree, backing up the hill to swing out and up, his long bony toes cutting into the blue sky then knifing into the water. He crawled onto the bank, shook his hair, and scrambled over to the trunk of the oak, where he shimmied easily to the uppermost branch.

Eddie stood straight up, hanging in the air like a hawk, and pointed his fingers to the sky. Without warning, he pitched forward—and here he seemed to pause like a memory before he vanished into the brown envelope of the pool. Andrew was still undressing on the bank when Eddie came out of the water and dropped onto the grass, hands on his knees, his chin lowered. He brushed his hands down his wet cheeks and narrow nose to his mouth. Andrew could see that Eddie's thoughts were elsewhere, but there was no getting out of it: he had to climb now, and he gripped onto the rough bark, which scraped at the inside of his knee. He wanted Eddie to look over and watch him climb, and eventually Eddie did look. Andrew stood on the branch and stared straight up. Instead of flying through the air like Eddie, he closed his eyes and stepped off the limb. His body lost its weight, his thoughts vanished. The cold stung his skin, and he came up for air, the water curling up against his chest. He was relieved it was over and thrilled as he looked up at the tree. It seemed like an unbelievable distance to have fallen.

Eddie floated out into the current of the stream, drifting on his back, and Andrew followed, turning around in the gentle rapids of the shallows. The treetops revolved as the flow pulled at his ankles, pushing at his neck, bearing him up and setting him down on slippery round stones that nudged his back. He thought of Eddie soaring down from the branch, and the image seemed to broaden in his sight until it covered the sky, making every day before and after partly this day, as if they had always known each other. Andrew held his breath and sank. Through the surface of the water, he watched the tree limbs and the sky pitch in the ripples. The cold numbed the skin of his fingers.

After some time, they floated against the bank and sat up together. Andrew reached over and briefly touched Eddie on the shoulder. Eddie looked down at Andrew's hand, and his expression softened as his cheeks colored.

"What happened to my sister?" Andrew asked. He was afraid to hear the answer, but he was sure Eddie was the only person who knew.

"She drowned," Eddie said with a low growl, and his lips closed over his horrible pale teeth, his skin reflected in the water turning suddenly yellow, his eyes black. Andrew jolted and buried his face in the stream and pushed away from the bank, holding his breath underwater for as long as he could. When he looked back, Eddie had already pulled on his shirt and was walking away.

Andrew heard the sound of the train approaching down the valley, and he ran panting to catch up with Eddie. He found him on the other side of the hill sitting on his haunches and tossing stones over a granite ledge that dropped twenty feet down to the tracks. Eddie closed his eyes and shook his head from side to side as if someone had told him a story that he knew wasn't true. Andrew crouched next to him and tried to catch his breath. The train came into view, louder, closer, the horn blasting, and the locomotive passed below them. The gust brushed Eddie's bangs to the side as he turned his head and opened his mouth to say something that Andrew couldn't hear over the roar of the engine.

Suddenly, Eddie clamped his eyes shut and his face balled into a knot. Something was wrong; Andrew didn't know what. Eddie stood up as the caboose passed and looked down at the tracks with his mouth open and his lower lip hanging dumb as a leaf.

In the silence after the train passed, Andrew would have expected some kind of warning, though there hadn't been any warning with Stephanie, not for the kind of thing she had been about to do. Eddie bared his teeth and his eyes turned to stones. He leapt off the ledge and into the sky—where, for a moment, his feet gripped the air—and Andrew thought Eddie might sail over the tracks to the opposite bank or keep rising above the trees. As clearly, though, as Andrew had known what would happen to Stephanie from the minute she arrived home from Portland, he knew that Eddie would fall, and he couldn't look.

He heard the awful crack of Eddie's bones—a sickening sound that was also, somehow, a relief. The sound of a body breaking. With Stephanie there had been no sound, just her empty room in the morning.

Eddie lay splayed on the tracks below, his chest slowly inflating. Andrew found a spot where the bank sloped and he scrambled down. Eddie's eyes opened halfway and stared beyond Andrew's face at the sky. His arm had snapped clean in half below the elbow, and the raw bone jutted out of his skin. Blood seeped from a cut in his head.

"What happened?" Eddie said, his face as open and pale as the moon in the daytime sky. A glaze of sweat covered his skin.

"You slipped," Andrew lied.

Eddie's eyes widened with fear; he scrambled to his feet and searched the ground around him as if he had dropped something. "Come on," he said and stumbled forward down the tracks.

Andrew caught up, and Eddie talked frantically about how they would do everything together now: swim after school, fish at the lake in Monmouth where his grandma lived, and play Frisbee down at the landing. They would meet outside Andrew's house in the morning and walk up to school together. Andrew didn't know why, but Eddie had chosen him.

When they reached the top of a rise, with a clear view of the steeple tops, Eddie abruptly stopped and looked down at his broken arm, and he gasped, his eyes closing over tears. Below the elbow his hand was twisted, and he shook his head either in disappointment or disbelief.

Eddie's knees buckled and Andrew tried to hold him up. He was too heavy, though, heavier than Andrew ever would have imagined, heavier, surely, than his sister. Andrew could no longer remember the sound of her voice, but as he tumbled under Eddie onto the tracks, he felt that the sudden and unfamiliar weight gave some shape to what Stephanie had left unsaid.

DARK ROOM

Just before the start, I walked up a back trail to the field and stood at the far edge of the finish line because I wanted to see my sister Melissa not run the big race. This was an important day for me because I was a mean person who wished that bad things would happen to those I loved. It was the year Amy Marsden grew an inch, making me the shortest kid in the sixth grade, and the year I told my friends Susan and Emma to "join the choir," which was a phrase we had for just the opposite. Their mothers called my mother and I got a lecture, which led to this being the year I stopped talking to my mother unless my father made me, and then I only did so as if she wasn't there, calling her "the woman."

I believed in God because I didn't think it was an option not to; I just didn't think, as my mother did, that He was Good. I had spent the week before the big race begging Him to keep Melissa from running. I also prayed that I would someday not ever see my family or anyone from Vaughn again. When this day arrived I would never, not even in my dreams, visit the town where I had grown up and miraculously escaped from to become the person I would be.

I knew Melissa was not at the race, but other people didn't: they must have thought she was warming up in the back parking lot, as she sometimes did, or stretching in the girls' locker room. Even if I had wanted to tell them she wasn't there, they would not have believed me because people believed what they wanted to believe, and they all wanted Melissa to win. People from Vaughn generally didn't win things, but Melissa was exactly the kind of person everyone would want to win: she was beautiful but humble, she was smart but meek. She believed God was Good, and even though she was too busty and wide-hipped to be a real runner (and didn't even join the cross-country team until her sophomore year), she had placed third at states in her first season. Coaches, parents, other runners, and writers for the *Valley Journal* all agreed that she had terrible form, running on the balls of her feet, and no strategy, leaving the start at full speed each time and not pacing herself. She finished each race with her eyes narrowed (sometimes, she said, she could no longer even see by the end), and her head tilted down as if she were listening to a reprimand she had heard many times before. She won these races through sheer exertion of will and because, people said, she had heart, whatever that meant.

William, the staff photographer for the *Valley Journal*, was one of the first people at the meet, pacing up and down in front of the crowd with his camera raised in the air, his belly pushing against his windbreaker. He photographed every sports event and was about as well known as someone could get in Vaughn for giving kids the only kind of fame they would ever see. He was anxious as he focused and refocused his lenses—more anxious, even, than Melissa's exboyfriend Doug, who leaned over the tape set up by the coaches and angled his mouth so she would hear his voice above all the others.

The girls lined up as a drizzle stung our cheeks. People craned their necks and squinted at the runners before turning to each other and shrugging—no Melissa. Some of them—especially the women, the other mothers—whispered to each other. William raised his camera but then let it drop against the neck strap. His face turned pale.

The pistol snap sent the runners forward in a wave under the gray November sky. Doug, the ex, gasped. Poor boy, I thought, though not out of compassion. He was poor. He didn't have a father and his mother mopped the floors at the Wharf. He was nice looking but too poor to look nice, Melissa's friend Becky had said.

Though it was nine in the morning, it might have been dusk, and as they disappeared down the path that snaked through the woods, Doug searched the leaders.

There were too many girls from other schools who looked the same, running away. Rain curled from branches in loping drops, but I was sure that in Doug's mind Melissa did not hear them hit the ground, nor did she hear the sound of her own breath, nor the heels of her sneakers over the packed mud, as she pulled ahead. Runners appeared in groups of twos and threes, their eyes drunk on exhaustion and stunned with the sudden glare of the metallic light as they pushed with the last of their will toward the line.

When Melissa's friend Merrill said Melissa hadn't come out of her house since the morning of the day before, William, the photographer, rushed over.

"What did you say?" he asked.

"Yesterday morning. She runs every morning, every morning,"—a fact everyone knew from the article in the *Journal*, for which William had done the photographs people raved about. His pictures of Old Vaughn Day were all right, but operating that one-touch camera couldn't be any harder, I thought, than spitting on your own shoe. And he couldn't see anything with a camera that I didn't already know: I knew Melissa thought Doug was a "total mistake," I knew she waxed her arm hairs and pictured herself (God knows why) someday married to a man who owned a Ford dealership, just as I knew that old Mrs. McDermott across the street mailed letters to herself from Augusta and slept in the nude. I knew most of what went on in our town (I was the short one standing with her arms crossed in the edge of people's vision), but on the morning of the big race I had no more idea than anyone why Melissa had locked herself in her room with the shades drawn and the lights out while our mother sat by the door speaking into the keyhole with her most conciliatory voice.

Melissa was still not answering when I got home. It was impossible not to defy our mother whose voice plucked at my nerves like the yowl of a cat in heat. But our poor mother did her best, trying to say it was nothing—teenage stuff—even though Melissa had never given in to melodrama before. She was a normal girl, our mother said, she did well in school, she had boyfriends (never too serious), she went to the movies, to dances, to parties, to football games, and always, for the last two years, she ran. She ran seventy-five miles a week.

Melissa's two best friends, Merrill and Becky, arrived in Merrill's boyfriend Billy's car. Billy stayed in the car while they knocked on the door.

"What's wrong? Why won't she come out?" Merrill said to me, but I didn't answer. I didn't talk to girls who went out with Billy. Someday Billy would regret that his father had ever given him that car, because it would have taken him too long to learn there was nothing else to him.

Our father paced in the kitchen; he didn't look so much angry as bewildered, until there was a knock and Doug's face leaned into the window of the front door.

Our father grabbed him hard by the shirt and Doug screamed Melissa's name as our father pushed him against the banister and screamed it again with such desperation that our father stepped back and looked at his hands, wondering what he had done.

Back then I used to think it was unbelievable how stupid people were. Our parents seemed to have no idea that (before she dumped him) Melissa had been sneaking out to see Doug almost every night. More than once, I had seen them park down the street and had seen him turn off the headlights to fall over in her direction.

Melissa had not had many boyfriends before Doug. He was the first semiserious one but only because he made it that way. She wasn't even sure she liked him that much (she told Merrill when I could hear them talking in her room through the radiator pipes). He was insistent, Melissa said, with his use of the word *love*, tossing it at her on a daily basis until she was fairly certain on at least a couple of occasions that it might be true. And she had to admit (as most people would if pressed) that it's not bad being loved by someone cute but poor, even if some of his people were mentally ill (his father was locked in his own room at the Augusta Mental Health Institute, a place so infamous for what my mother called its "dirt basement ways" that perfectly sane people visiting their unfortunate relatives were known to have fallen apart behind its walls and never come out).

The phone started ringing before my father let go of Doug and it did not stop. People who had been at the race, or whose children or parents or brothers and sisters and cousins had been there, called to find out what was wrong. Our father picked up the phone the first two times and yelled louder than he should have that he didn't *know* what was wrong. He was about to pick it up a third time when our mother came down and unplugged it from the wall.

No one was thinking about William, the photographer, except me. I had seen him drive away after the race. At that time of day, his wife Miriam would have been out for a walk. She couldn't go very far, in the seventh month, without having to pee, so she would have stopped to use the bathroom at Boyton's Market. She had mentioned to her friend, Mrs. Pomeroy, a teacher at my school (who passed everything on to my mother), that her husband was worried about money. Miriam had also been a teacher (my favorite) at my school until that fall, when she quit because of the baby.

William had photographed Melissa dozens of times at races, but I did not think anything of it until he parked down the street from our house the night of the race. I might have thought he had come for me because, as usual, I expected something catastrophic to happen to me, something so awful that for generations people would close their eyes and shake their heads whenever my name was mentioned. But no one ever came for me. My light was off, my window as dark as William's car. I would not have seen him except for the light shining from Melissa's room spreading out into the road. Melissa could not stand to be off her feet for long (today she is a nurse in Augusta), and I heard her pacing in front of her window, her foot landing with an ugly clump on every other step as if she had a cane or a wooden leg. William slid over into the passenger seat of his car and pressed his face against the glass, looking up at her window.

William had never spoken to me, though I had heard him speak. I had heard everyone's voice at one time or another, and I hated his most of all. I hated him as much as I loved his wife Miriam. I hated him because he had made her pregnant so she no longer taught at my school and I couldn't see her every day as I had before. I hated the look of his face, so thin and pointed at the chin, with a cleft that changed shape like a mouth when he spoke. Everyone was surprised when he got into art school in Boston with a full scholarship. I had no memory of him before he left Vaughn, but I remembered hating him the first time I saw him when he came back with the beautiful woman who was not from Vaughn: the "Boston girl" people called her. I didn't care if she was a pagan witch; I loved her outfits and her pale hands and the absolutely pure elegance of what I later figured out was nothing but a Southie accent.

William liked to tell the story to people he worked with at the paper (once to my father and other men at my house while they all sat drinking beer in the backyard and I listened from the kitchen window) of how he and Miriam first met in a bar on Newbury Street where he spontaneously broke into "My Lagan Love" after having a few too many boilermakers and noticed her sitting by herself, waiting for a friend (a date, it turned out) who never showed up. He asked her to dance; she declined. He persisted until the whole bar called for her to join him, though in her account (William admitted to my father) the bar was empty except for her, the bartender, and William and his two friends. When she moved to push him away, he saw the series of deep scars over the top of her right hand extending up into her sleeve. He stopped, stared at her face for a long moment, and said he was very sorry for bothering her while slightly drunk but that she really was so beautiful. He would be enormously grateful, he said, if she would dance with him just once because it was his birthday. She said of course it wasn't his birthday. He waltzed her across the floor, though according to her version she helped him stagger back to his chair while he sang "Cavan Girl" and "Molly Malone" in honor of his old grandmamma.

To me William was old, like my parents, part of a vast race I would never join. Miriam was another being entirely. When she still taught at my school, she wore skirts made of the same material as people's fancy head scarves. Her long, perfectly straight hair reached all the way down to the small of her back.

I could never understand why Miriam agreed to move to Vaughn from Boston. Susan and Emma had said it was obvious that she was so in love with William that she would move anywhere, even to the town where we lived, which no one moved to unless they had lived there before and had no choice but to come back. William had come back by choice, though, quitting college in Boston six months short of graduation and not long after he met Miriam. Apparently, no one explained to him that it's easy to resent someone who leaves and impossible to respect anyone who comes back.

Eventually, William started the car and drove away, but I did not sleep. Instead of going to school the next morning, I went to sit on the library steps across the street from the apartment where William and Miriam lived. I wanted to speak to him; I had no idea why, nor any idea what I would say. My palms burned red, which says something about how my cheeks must have looked. People talk about seeing red, but when I was that angry everything in town looked like a pencil drawing to me, black on white.

It was still early when he drove by me, but instead of heading to the paper, he pushed down his left blinker and climbed Litchfield Road, rising up out of the valley. The dampness of the river flowed through the air as I stood to watch him. I didn't know where he was going at first, but then I remembered that on the morning before the big race, there was a car accident down the road from where Melissa usually ran. William would have seen Melissa as he drove home from shooting the wreck. They knew each other from the races. Now he was headed back to the spot where the low fog collected on the pine needles and oak leaves, where he had veered off the road and pulled her into the car and the two of them fought with two or three times their strength. She tried to move her arms, but he held them down; she tried to scream, but he covered her mouth and pinned her across the front seat. He needed both hands to hold her down, she was so strong. Her legs, her runner's legs, kicked at his legs. All the freedoms she had previously taken for granted, even her sight and her thoughts, were suffocated by his face bearing down on her. Her clothes stripped away, her pale skin white with terror.

I waited outside his apartment for him to come back, and when he did, I stood but didn't know what to do. Miriam came out onto the porch. Neither of them saw me, though I was in plain sight.

"You were supposed to be here an hour ago," she said. She stared impassively at his face, and he stared back, looking into her eyes.

"Remember?" she said.

"Of course I remember," he said, and went inside.

I wanted to warn Miriam—everyone knew she had suffered enough with what had happened in

Philadelphia—but the words wouldn't come out of my mouth. The thought of anything bad happening to her again was too much for me to bear, too much for any of us in Vaughn to bear. I sat down and hugged myself as the door closed behind William.

Miriam would no longer talk about it, but when she first moved to town, people asked her about the scars on her arm and prodded her to tell them what had happened. I first heard it from my friend Becky (who had heard it from her mother, who had overheard Miriam telling Evan at Boyton's) a month after Miriam started teaching in my school. At first I didn't believe Becky, who said if I didn't I could go over and ask Miriam, who stood in the corner of the playground with her chin pulled into her chest and her arms crossed. No one expected me to be this brave. It was late fall, almost too cold already on this day to snow, and Miriam was not dressed right. She was never dressed right for the weather, but this, along with her long hair and the hardness of her mouth from which we never once heard an unkind word either on the playground or in the classroom, was why we loved her. She had the glow by now of a war hero or the kind of apostle we had been told about every Sunday in the priest's same droning voice. Becky and some of the other girls watched as I went up to Miriam and asked her if it was true.

She squatted down with her arms wrapped around her knees just as my friends and I did, huddling together when it was too cold to endure another second of recess.

"What have you heard?" she said.

I froze and couldn't say. Even though she knew what I wanted to ask, she would not help me until I finally pointed at the scars on her arm and managed at least to open my mouth. My mitten had slipped off my hand and hung by its tether from my sleeve.

"It probably is true," she said, "if you heard it."

For some reason, I forgot to stop pointing at her arm. In the cold, my fingers turned pink and pale. Then she did something that gave me for a brief time the only kind of fame I would ever know, for kids would talk about me for the rest of the year as Miriam's favorite: she leaned forward in a rush and wrapped her arms around me so that my face was buried in her beautiful soft sweater. She smelled of the ocean on a hot day, and her lips burned my ear.

"It's true," she said. "Whatever you heard is true."

In what she called her first life, Miriam moved from South Boston to Philadelphia with her fiancé and taught at one of the downtown elementary schools. They lived near Temple and planned to get pregnant when he finished law school that spring. They didn't have enough money to eat at restaurants, but they often ate in the park at dusk. One fall night they were on their way to the park when a man came up behind them and grabbed her fiancé by the shoulder to spin him around and push him against the wall. Miriam opened her mouth to scream, but panic overcame her voice. It was a boy, no bigger than her, with yellow eyes and burning red cheeks, wielding a knife as he spat demands she couldn't understand.

"Here, here," her fiancé yelled and dropped his backpack. The boy didn't seem to care about that and pressed the knife against his chest. Her fiancé fumbled for his wallet, but his hands shook as the boy's rage grew. His demands had turned into a drumroll of curses that increased in rhythm and volume until his face exploded with anguish and he stabbed at her fiancé's chest. Miriam tried to pull the boy off, but he seemed to have the strength of someone twice his size. She forced her way between them and took the blows of the knife on her forearm and wrist until the boy simply stopped as suddenly as he had attacked and ran down the street. The blade had struck her fiancé's shoulder, chest, and neck. She shoved her hand over the gash in his neck and turned around as a car passed, the passenger in the front seat staring at them with a blank face. She waved at the second car with her free hand, but this one did not stop either. She tried to lift him under the armpits, but she couldn't get him off the ground without taking her hand off his neck. Eventually, she managed to drag him into the middle of the street where a car had to stop, but it was too late.

A week and a half after the incident, the boy who had attacked them scaled the side of a public housing complex and at two a.m. entered the fifth-story window of an elderly Jewish couple's apartment. He raged through, overturning drawers and tables looking for money. When the old man tried to write a check, the boy stabbed him thirty times and then kicked the old woman to death. Police found him on the couple's couch watching television and eating ice cream from their freezer.

When my mother heard this story, she said it was exactly the kind of thing that only happened in cities, but I knew it could happen here, too.

After a short time, William came out of their apartment and walked down Second Street. I followed a block behind. Mrs. Eliot, one of the high school guidance counselors, drove by in her husband's truck and raised her hand from the steering wheel. Usually she drove the old station wagon with her kids buckled in the backseat. Mrs. Kemper, who worked at Boyton's, stood out back having a cigarette and staring at her feet. William walked up the steps of the newspaper.

I was there, waiting as it started to rain, when he came out fifteen minutes later. He stopped and stared right at me for a long minute, and I stared right back. I forced myself not to blink and dared him to speak. He shook his head, as if disagreeing with what I was thinking, and then started home through the rain by a shortcut down the hill between the rectory and the Methodist church. He paused on the slope next to the library overlooking his apartment, where Miriam worked at the counter in the kitchen window. Soaked through to the skin, I looked with him through the window at the blurred features of Miriam's face. She might have been anyone, except that I knew it was she from the way she kept her hair pushed to one side. I thought that whatever he had done to my sister—who wouldn't get the scholarship because she hadn't won the race, who wouldn't go to college—he would do to Miriam next.

I ran and didn't stop until I made it to Boyton's, where I called my mother. When she finally pulled up in the car, I tried to get her to do something.

"We have to save Miriam, we have to tell Chuck Sheldon," I yelled at my mother, who only shook her head, telling me she had enough to deal with at the moment without worrying about where I had been all day. Melissa had come out of her room barely able to walk, with bad stress fractures in her right leg. "Poor girl," my mother said, "she should have let up a long time ago. She must have been running in pain for months. Now they won't heal, the doctor said, for a long time, and when they do, she probably won't be able to run. She counted on that scholarship."

At home, Melissa reeled around the house (my father said) like a drunken bear.

"My life is over. It's over!" she screamed, and I burst into tears before collapsing on the floor. I had wanted Melissa to miss the race, I had wanted her to fail.

"It's his fault! He did it," I screamed and pulled at my hair until my mother held my arms at my sides. "I thought I hated you, but I don't!" I managed to say to Melissa before I broke into sobs again. I loved her and now it was too late because her life was ruined. Melissa wrapped her arms around my head. She told me everything would be fine and that she loved me, too. But I knew she was lying—everything would not be fine and she couldn't really love me. My heart was too hard.

I said William's name under my breath and thought she nodded in response, though probably she didn't hear, or she thought I said something else.

"Now stop this," our mother said. "Your life is not ruined. It's only your shins."

"Can you believe she said *only my shins*?" Melissa said.

"What did he do to you? What did he do?" I screamed.

"Who?"

I didn't believe her. I didn't believe anyone. I ran to my room, locked myself inside, and would not come out for dinner. My father knocked and said they had all been tried enough, but I said I would not come out until they all admitted I was right. He said he didn't know what I was talking about. Instead of pleading, my mother threatened to ground me if I didn't come out. When my mother left, Melissa came to the door.

"I'm sorry," she whispered. "Please, please, I'm sorry. Just come out." She sobbed, but still I would not open the door.

"Why don't you tell me the truth? When you tell me the truth, I'll come out," I said, staring at the doorknob.

"The truth about what?" she said.

"About William."

She was silent, so I opened the door. But she was gone.

"I know what happened out on Litchfield Road," I yelled through her door.

"I had shin splints," she yelled back.

"You got in the car with him." She didn't answer. I had thought that he pulled her into the car, but of course Melissa knew William, had spoken to him weeks before when she was interviewed for the paper. I had seen them stand next to each other after a race as the sweat dried on her cheeks; he said her name to her and asked her questions about the team after the interview was over. Then he asked her to pose in front of the field and rest her hands on her hips while he raised the lens to his face and snapped the shutter. He was on his way back from shooting the accident when he saw her walking along the side of the road with a limp—that much, the shin splints, was true.

More than anything, I wanted to know what William had felt when he saw Melissa alone on the road. I wanted to feel compelled like that—to be taken over. He almost drove away from her but couldn't. He squeezed his eyes shut but saw her face in the blood black; his hands froze, his breath seized, he couldn't speak. He didn't want to be there, he had to be there, and this was something no one would understand, he thought. After he pulled over, Melissa leaned her head through his open window, the wet strands of her hair brushing his cheeks as he closed his eyes. "I'm freezing," Melissa said to him, and rushed over to the passenger side to open the door. That's when it happened, and because she had agreed to get in the car, she blamed herself.

I pounded on Melissa's door and demanded that she come out and tell me the truth about William. I could see what had happened in my thoughts, but I had to hear it from her. I *had* to know.

I sat down outside Melissa's door and said I would not move. I would not eat or breathe. Finally, if she didn't tell me, I would show her and the rest of them— I would stop loving them.

I realized as I said it that I had always wanted an excuse to stop feeling and thinking—to be nothing but a pane of glass in the open air—and in many ways, this fantasy has come true for me. I am the librarian, here in Vaughn, the custodian of several thousand books. Hundreds of them pass through my hands each year, though I don't read them anymore. The kids come down here after school, but they don't check out the books, or look between the covers. They don't see me just as they don't see the books. They creep back into the stacks and slip their hands up under sweaters and shirts to feel the heat of each other's bodies. Or they sit at the long oak tables and stare at each other, occasionally bursting out with laughter that echoes high into the rafters—like half the buildings in this town, the library used to be a church.

"You got in the car and he attacked you," I whispered into the keyhole of Melissa's door.

"He didn't attack me," she hissed.

"But you just wanted a ride home."

Her door opened a crack, and I saw her lips. She whispered so our mother wouldn't hear. "No," she said. "No."

I thought I finally had my answer—she had crossed the seat to him, her pupils expanding like drops of blood in a basin of water.

"But it's his fault—it's his fault?" I said.

Melissa's door closed and the lock turned. She would say no more.

That winter, the winter after Melissa missed the big race, was the worst winter I had known. Melissa said if I didn't stop asking her questions, I would no longer be her sister, and I believed her. It snowed almost all the time, and when it didn't snow, it was too cold to snow, the wind coming down like a fist from up north, drawing a sheath of ice east over the river. I had pneumonia because no matter what my mother said, I always left the house with my hair wet and no hat or coat. I couldn't sleep and wouldn't eat. My fever burned until the plows scraping up Central Street seemed to dig through my head. For a long time I thought I would die in the middle of the night and my parents would find me in the morning with frost-rimmed nostrils. I didn't die, though, and Melissa's stress fractures healed enough for her to walk to school with her friends.

Miriam's baby was born a boy, Andrew. On those winter nights, I pictured William rising to look down at his son's limbs pumping in the dark. While Miriam slept, he would cradle Andrew in his arms for three or four hours waiting for him to fall asleep. But I knew that even during those brief respites, when Andrew quieted and slowly uncurled his fists in silence, William could still hear his son scream his one indecipherable note, his only bleating message.

In the spring, William came to photograph our school. Vaughn Elementary had scored first in the region in the standardized test we took every year. Our picture was going to be in the paper. We filed onto the playground where the teachers tried to arrange us in three rows: the taller kids in the back, and the smallest ones, like me, in the front. I was sullen, sitting crosslegged with a bunch of third graders while my friends held hands somewhere behind me. William arrived with his tripod and camera and began to set up while we shivered. He seemed in no hurry as he adjusted his equipment. Only when he looked through the lens and focused did his back stiffen, and only I knew why. He returned to his bag of equipment for a light meter, which he pointed at us like a weapon, and looked at me from around the side of his camera. This time he could not turn away, his eyes flashing white and his mouth open as he stared right at me. He lowered his head behind the camera again as I was brought to my feet by an urgency moving through me. I could no more have stopped myself from raising my finger than stop a train. Mrs. Douglas yelled for me to sit down, but I walked forward while pointing at the lens of William's camera. Right before I reached him, he slipped on a patch of ice and flew back as if from the force of my accusation: "You, you, you!" I said as he tried to stand but slipped again. "I'm telling what you did to my sister. Her life is over now!" I screamed. I held him down with my eyes until Mrs. Douglas lifted me up and ushered me to the principal's office, where I waited for Mr. Wheeler's heels to snap down the hall. In my mind, I dared him to punish me in the worst way he knew how. I might be sent home, they might call my mother, but that's all. Only after he straightened his tie and swept aside the few strands of hair covering his pate, as hideous, I thought, as a dog's belly, did he ask what on earth had gotten into me. I wanted to tell about William, but I was no longer sure what to tell, and I was sure Melissa would never speak to me again if I did. I didn't care about the rest of them, but I needed my sister.

"I don't know," I said, sitting upright, as tall as I could in the low chair. Just the thought of William made me want to hold my hand against a wood stove. I couldn't explain to Mr. Wheeler any more than I could explain to myself that William filled me with hatred and terror because he was the person I might become. He had tumbled into the bottomless hole of a single fixation, Melissa, and it was just a matter of time before the same thing happened to me with someone or something else. Only I wasn't going to let it happen. I promised myself at that moment that I wouldn't let it.

A few months after William took that picture of our school, he disappeared without a word to anyone. He went downriver to Gardner to shoot a warehouse fire and never came back. William's mother helped with Andrew and assured Miriam and everyone else that she knew her son; the boy would come back. When he didn't, however, come back after several months, and his car was found abandoned in Boston, William's mother insisted on a service at Saint Catherine's, where William and Andrew had been baptized. No body was found, but the minister agreed, even though I think he suspected, as I did, that William was still out there somewhere, vanished but not gone.

Most of the town walked up the hill to the church that day: William's friends from the paper, his cousins, my parents, Melissa, and Mr. Dawson, who had been a friend of William's father. Of course Miriam was there, too, in a black dress with silk ruffles that Sara Mills had borrowed from her sister, who had also lost a husband young. Miriam cried the way people sometimes do in books, without making a sound or moving her lips, her frozen complexion crested with a black lace hat, her eyes framed by purple rings. At the end of the service, she quietly bowed. It was the end of a summer Sunday, and Mr. Dawson had set up food from his store outside. People filed out of the gray church, collected around the tables, and stood with lowered heads picking at the rectangular ham and chicken sandwiches. One of the deacons had planted roses along the walkway, and in the flannel gown of the August air people seemed as shy around each other as if they had never met.

On her way home, carrying her son in her arms, Miriam passed by where I stood under an old maple at the far edge of the church lawn, and I told her I was sorry for her loss. She looked up and said thank you, though I could see she was not sorry he was gone. None of us were.

A FAIR CHANCE

Pete stood in front of his parents' house clapping his gloved hands together in the falling snow. For the first time in the six months Pete had been working for him, Jack was late, and when he did appear from around the corner in his old Ford Ranger, he had a man the size of a moose in the seat next to him. Jack was busy shouting at the man, and he showed no sign of slowing. The passenger door flew open while they were still moving, and the truck spun in a slow circle, passing right in front of Pete. They came to a halt in the middle of the road facing the wrong direction, and Jack leaned over the steering wheel with his eyes closed. The man next to him looked at Pete and pulled a smile across his face as if his mouth were a trigger and his dark, closely set eyes the double barrel of a shotgun.

Pete threw his gear in the bed with the saws and gas and tried to squeeze in next to the man's knees, which folded into his chest and pressed against the dash. Up close, the man looked like the largest kid Pete had ever seen.

"You probably heard of me," he said, looking at Pete out of the corner of one eye.

"Heard of you?"

"I'm the one that killed that guy up in Bangor— drove a hammer right through the back of his melon."

Jack slowly shook his head.

"I'm just playin'. But there was a guy up in the county done his mother that way—with a friggin' hammer. Believe that?"

Obviously, this was Jack's son, Doug. Pete had heard of Doug, who had grown up with an aunt in Gardner, where he was known to have thrown a kid out of a moving car. The dashboard heater blasted against Doug's tattered snowmobile suit, filling the cab with the smell of rotten venison. Pete only wished Jack had told him he was going to hire his son, though it wouldn't have changed anything. After the accident, Jack was the only person around willing to give him a job.

They passed between low white hills and distant gray tree lines. Jack headed west out of Vaughn toward a new stand outside Eutis, not far from the Maine-Quebec border. Pete hadn't seen it yet, but according to Jack it was supposed to have a slope of ten degrees, no more, up from the road; there was very little birch or alder and no stumpage to the owner, as long as they pum-yarded, burning the brush as they worked. The owner, some guy from Massachusetts, was going to put a hunting camp in and just wanted part of it cleared. They'd get a lot of sixteen-fours out of those trees for boards, the rest for stud, Jack had said. Even if they paid someone to skid the logs to the road, they'd come out double their usual take, and Jack was going to give him a share this time instead of paying him by the hour. Jack thought he was taking Pete on as a partner, but if Pete could bank enough, this would be his last job. After a year of sleeping up in his old bedroom and eating his mother's eggs across from his father every morning, he could leave Vaughn for good and move down to Portland.

The land rose toward the White Mountains. The snow was deeper up here, and the sky lightened as they passed through Eutis, turned down a dirt road, and after a few minutes, stopped. A southerly breeze moved through the woods, and though it wasn't even April yet, the air was warmer than it had been since last September. They all stood next to the truck looking at the sky and up the slope of the hill where they had to go. It didn't seem like a 10 percent grade, not from down here. Fifteen, at least, or twenty. Doug tied the arms of his snowsuit around his waist and, following Jack's lead, Pete stripped down to his T-shirt. One way or another, Pete thought, Doug was going to cut into his share. There were only two saws, and he sure as hell wasn't going to get stuck yarding all day on a sucker's cut.

There was deep sloppy snow at the bottom, but up above it dried out in the duff. Jack set his load down and waved his hand to the west. Pete dropped to his knees, filled the saw with gas and chain oil, tightened the chain on the bar, and headed out half a dozen paces to start limbing the large pines and spruce while Jack walked in a widening circle around their gear, blazing most of the bigger trees with his axe. If a tree didn't need to come down, he wasn't going to take it down just to make it easier to fell the big ones. Jack was supposed to be one of the best in the woods, the great-grandson of a Finnish stonecutter from Hurricane Island, who used to timber cruise for Great Northern up in the Kingdom before he got sick of working for people and became a small-time jobber between the Saint John and the Dead Rivers. Jack would do all the felling after Pete and Doug ran the saw up and down the outside of the trunks, stripping off the lower limbs. Pete was sure Doug knew not to limb pulling the saw up (the chain could easily snag and pitch the bar back into your face), but he did it anyway. Jack took the saw from Doug and face cut and back cut out a wedge so there would be no split in the butt of the log. Pete waited for the first tree to fall. For some reason, no one had done any high-grading here over the years. Everywhere else they had worked over the last six months had been stripped of the best wood every twenty-five years for the last hundred and fifty, leaving the cull of each generation to reproduce for the next.

Pete felt an unexpected excitement as he took his finger off the trigger of the saw and looked up at the long straight trunks hurling through the pale sky. They'd be able to use all the log—no blue stain or red rot. These weren't old growth trees, but old growth was often useless—spike topped and full of heart rot. These trees were tall and straight, in their prime. There was some hackmatack up the hill mixed in with useless popple, but hardly any puckerbrush to fight through. The owner had no idea what kind of wood he was giving away, and Pete felt a certain pleasure in his knowledge of the woods, though it had been hard won in the last year.

Jack had taken Pete to his first AA meeting, and a few months later given him work. Pete didn't want to tell Jack he was leaving after this job. He felt guilty about it, because Jack would just end up going it alone, and he was too old for that. Maybe Doug would keep working with the old man, though Pete doubted it.

A shudder passed up the trunk of the first tree and the top swayed for a moment before falling along the path Jack had chosen for it. Pete dragged the bar of the saw along the flanks of the trunk, stripping off the limbs. At four lengths of the saw and the orange tail sticking off the back, he bucked a log at sixteen-four and rolled it over with his heel to limb the underside. Doug picked up the logs and tossed them into piles as if they weighed no more than two-by-fours. At this pace, they could level the stand in three weeks, maybe a month.

"This is great for me," Doug yelled above the noise of the saw. "I need the money, and I need the money bad. There's a guy starting a garage over in Londonderry. I need a thousand bucks to go in with him. He's the surgeon, I'm the body man."

Pete just stared at him for a minute. It was Jack's unspoken rule that they keep the talk to a minimum until it was time for coffee at ten thirty, and Pete liked the rules, he realized. He liked the predictability. Doug was the opposite of that.

"Hey," Doug said. "You get high? You do, don't you?"

Pete glanced over at Jack, who was busy sizing up a big spruce.

"I'm gonna score a dime bag when we're done with this day. I'll have to get a ride up to Augusta for it, though. You got wheels?"

Pete shook his head and turned back to the tree, hoping Doug would shut up. The saw turned off (he had hit the kill switch by accident, which he often did when he wasn't paying attention), and Doug was right there again.

"He doesn't know half the shit I've been up to, Mr. AA," he said, looking over at his father. "Let me take her for a spin." He grabbed the saw away from Pete, holding it in his left hand and yanking on the cord with his right—another suicidal habit. He started limbing one of the trees Jack had felled, but he left two-inch stubs and got bored halfway up the trunk and turned to the base of a standing tree. Pete started to throw the limbs into piles they could burn later. After he finished, he looked around and saw a fifty-foot hairball of a juniper smash through the upper limbs of a spruce to hang up fifteen feet over Jack's head. Jack stopped his saw, marched over to Doug, and started cursing at the top of his lungs.

"You," he said, pointing his finger at Doug, "come with me." Doug made a conspiratorial face at Pete and trundled after his father, giving an exaggerated wag to his blocky head. Jack was a hard driver but fair. Even in his cups, Pete's mother had said, Jack had never been a beater. "That's the one thing I know, from Phyllis herself, before she died. But when he was still drinking," his mother had said, "he would take off for weeks, sometimes months at a time, and he never had any money with him when he came out of the woods, he wasn't there when Doug was born, and he wasn't there when Phyllis was sick. Everyone knows he never even so much as said happy birthday to that boy after the cancer took Phyllis. Doug lived with that awful woman, Phyllis's sister, until Jack got sober, and by then, I dare say, it was too late. But ever since Jack got sober, he's done everything he could." Pete had heard people in AA talk of how Jack was always lending money to Doug, giving him cars and, in one case, his own truck, which Doug drove into a graveyard and wrapped around a power pole.

Jack set Doug up pulling the brush together and trudged back over to Pete with his lips pulled straight and tight. He gave Pete his saw back, and they went to work limbing and bucking to log length, some to stud length, Doug piling them up. The noise of the saw was the closest thing to total silence. As he often did, Pete thought he heard a voice in the whine of the blade cutting through a trunk. He stopped to look around and remembered again what had happened.

Pete knew that a lot of people in Vaughn said the accident was exactly what they had expected of him, even though Jen had been the one driving. When he and Jen went up to Orono together to the state university, her parents tried to get her to break up with him, saying he had been no good from the beginning. At fifteen, he was kicked off the basketball team. A kid from Coney fouled him just before a layup, and when the ref didn't call it, Pete cuffed the kid in the side of the head. They went at it in the middle of the floor for a minute before the refs pulled them apart and threw Pete out of the game. Pete waited for the kid in the parking lot and jumped him from behind. "What kind of kid jumps someone from behind?" Coach Dawson asked his parents. Then his senior year he was caught cheating on a math test. He would have been expelled if his mother had not pressured his father, the senior math teacher, to step in. Pete failed the course but graduated anyway, and everyone knew why. When he went to AA after the accident, people said (Jen's father said, anyway) that Pete hadn't really changed—he only went to meetings to get everyone off his back. Jen's father ran the branch of the Gardner Savings Bank; he could tell people the river ran north and they would believe it.

The first time Pete went back to drinking, a week after he started AA, everyone knew about it the next day. The bartender at the Wharf had thrown him out at nine thirty at night. AA was anonymous but his drinking wasn't (after leaving the Wharf, he had walked up and down Water Street yelling at the dark windows of the shops). The people in AA took him back and told him to keep trying. They said the same thing two weeks later when he went out again, but after the third time people stopped coming up to him at meetings. They looked away when he walked into the room; they had given up on him, all except Jack who never once asked why Pete had gone back out.

"When you come to pick me up, if I'm not there I guess you know where I am," Pete said to him once.

"Fair enough," Jack said.

Jack kept taking Pete to meetings, and Pete kept going because he would have to move out of his parents' house right away if he stopped—that was the agreement. His parents said he wasn't trying hard enough; his father said Pete was trying to break his mother's heart. Pete was trying, though. It didn't help that his mother could barely look at him when he came home at night.

It didn't take long for Doug to look bored. He stretched his arms out and craned his neck, surveying the trees with the same vacant smile he had been wearing all morning. He was stoned, Pete realized. Doug shouted something at his father, who shook his head that he couldn't hear. He shouted again and again until both Pete and Jack turned their saws off.

"Have you seen my butts?" Doug said, still shouting.

"Jesus, Mary, and Joseph—how the fuck would I know?"

"Did you see them in the truck?"

"Did I see your cigarettes in the truck? Why don't you keep them with you?"

"Cause I'm trying to quit."

Pete didn't want to say anything, but he could see the outline of the pack in the pocket of Doug's snowmobile suit.

"Go down there and look yourself, and when you come back bring the extra gas and the tea."

Jack sat down on a stump and ran both hands over the top of his head.

"Jesus, that boy's gaumy," he said after Doug had disappeared below. "I shouldna let him come. He's saving money to move out west, he said, work on the oil rigs in Wyoming. It's something different every time."

"He's strong," Pete said.

"I had to say yes, when he called," Jack said, looking up at Pete. His eyes seemed uncertain. "I had to give him another shot, despite what happened last time."

"What happened last time?" Pete asked, but Jack didn't answer.

Doug climbed back up the hill and stopped at one of the brush piles to turn the gas can upside down into the branches. The better part of five gallons soaked into the ground before Pete could get Jack to turn and look. Doug snapped off a match and tossed it into the pile. The fireball that rose into the trees knocked Doug onto his ass. He howled with pleasure and leapt to his feet.

"You see that?" Doug yelled.

There was still enough snow and slush around the pile to keep it from spreading, but it was burning so hot Pete could feel it on his face.

"We don't burn until the end of the day," Jack said, clearly trying to restrain himself. "And we don't waste the gas. Use newspaper."

"I was just trying to help."

"If you want to help, start histing those logs over there and don't touch the gas and matches. You got that?" he said, and when Doug didn't answer: "You hear me?"

"Yes! Jesus. I don't see why we gotta burn brush anyway."

"*Yhteishyva*," Jack said.

"Finnish wisdom," Doug grumbled and went off to the row of logs Jack had left.

"And because the owner wants it done, and the owner pays your salary. All right," Jack said, nodding at Pete.

The high sun shone through the hole they had cut in the sky and warmed them as if it were June. Jack and Pete took off their T-shirts. It was too early in the season yet for midges and black flies, but robins and whip-poor-wills flitted through the air. Squirrels cut paths along branches from tree to tree, moss dampened the toes of their boots and the tattered cuffs of their cutting pants. They ate while they worked, forgetting the coffee. A day like this, a forerunner of spring, made the woods seem frantic with anticipation for the coming season, and Pete couldn't keep from thinking about the kind of life he would set up for himself in Portland, where no one knew anything about him. He would find an apartment up on the east end, on Munjoy Hill, with a view of the bay. Things were still cheap up there, people said, and it was walking distance to downtown where he'd get some kind of job in a restaurant. Something to start with until he found a better position. Part of him would miss the woods, the smell of timber, running his hand along the defined grain of a juniper stump, and the crisp air filled with scorched sap. He had better things in mind, though. He would always associate Jack with Vaughn, and with Jen, and the accident. The longer he stayed in Vaughn, the more he felt time running out.

Doug and Jack avoided each other for a couple hours until Doug pulled limbs away from a big pine Jack was still bucking, and they started getting in each other's way. The chain caught Jack's pants and cut open the cloth below the knee, leaving a thin red slice in the skin.

Jack shut the saw off and motioned for Pete to come gas up. Pete filled his three-quarters full before the can went dry.

"I thought I told you to bring up the full can of gas," Jack said. He couldn't speak to Doug without tension and frustration boiling in his voice.

"That is the full can," Doug said. "The other one's empty."

"What happened to all the gas?" Jack said, and looked at the pile of scorched limbs where Doug had started the fire. "You didn't dump that whole can onto the pile? Tell me you didn't."

"I didn't either."

"Then what happened to all the friggin' gas?"

Doug knitted his brow and ground his jaw.

"I don't know," he whined, his face twisting like a child's until an idea seemed to come over him. "I'll go get some more," he said. "That store's just a few miles down the road. Five minutes. Faster'n you guys burn through a tank."

He smiled at Pete and nodded a few times, as if they had some prearranged agreement.

Jack mulled it over for a moment, sitting on his heels and pulling his finger through the pine needles. "Arright," he said. "Hurry up. Couple hours before dark."

"I need the keys."

Jack dug the keys out of his pocket and handed them over.

"I ain't got no money."

"Course you ain't," Jack said and pulled out a twenty.

Doug took off running down the hill, and they started up the saws. Either because Doug was gone or because the air was warm or because the wood was perfect, they worked faster than they ever had before, the trees tumbling and blocking up into neat symmetrical piles, the sky opening up more with every minute. A great spruce slammed into the ground and shivered. Pete loved to see them go down. It felt like progress. Maybe this was how the people who first came here, the pioneers, felt, when everything was covered with trees. With the logs spread out, some in piles and some lying where they had fallen, it was hard to tell how many cords they had cut. Jack worked tirelessly, even frantically, the sweat running down the channels on his narrow back as if it were summer already.

Pete was hot, too; the salt dripped down into the corners of his mouth. After a long winter of cutting in five below, it was finally spring, and for the first time since the accident, Pete felt there was a shot for him. He thought about Portland again, allowing himself to imagine the people he would meet at bars. He would have to go to bars, because there was nowhere else to meet people. He wouldn't mention Vaughn or Jen or any of it when he got there. He would be the person he decided to be.

He had more than just his own life to get away from. Pete's father had been ambitious—at least that was how Pete's religious mother described it. Obsessed, Pete would say, with becoming principal of the high school. For years he had talked of little else, encouraging Pete's mother to befriend the wives of people on the school board and getting her to host parties for them. When the long-time principal, Mr. Cunningham, retired four years after he was supposed to, his father finally had what he knew would be his one shot. He wasn't even interviewed, though, and in retaliation, he gave an angry speech at a school assembly. His father never seemed obviously drunk after that, but his eyes were always watery and stunned, fixing on one object in the room after another as if he might spot at any moment the door through which he would flee. Pete's father was no doubt driven by the shame of what had happened to his own father, who was caught embezzling thousands of dollars from the American Legion Post where he had been the treasurer for years. His wife, Pete's grandmother, had to sell the car she had bought after thirty-five years of nursing, in order to pay back her husband's debt. All of this happened, as everything did, in full view of the whole town.

Pete didn't realize it had started to rain until his saw quit. The sky had turned matte gray and the woods had darkened in the shadows. Jack worked on as the rain soaked his hair, and eventually his saw quit, too. Then it started to sleet. Pete found his wet T-shirt on a pile of wood and pulled it over his head. Jack walked toward him lugging the chain saw. His face was drawn and narrow, his mouth hanging open with steam pouring out.

"We bucked a lot of board today," he said, grinning. He didn't seem to grasp yet that it was sleeting, and that it was cold. "Where's Doug?" he said, setting the saw down and scanning the woods.

"He never came back," Pete said as he started to shake. The rest of their clothes were in the truck, with Doug and the matches.

"He never came back," Jack said flatly. As always, Pete waited for what Jack would say they should do next, and normally Jack never hesitated. Now, though, he set his jaw and stared listlessly down the hill. He looked straight up into the sky and closed his eyes as the rain and sleet hit his face. By the time he finally turned to Pete again, his cheeks had turned white.

"Jack," Pete said.

Jack opened his mouth, looked down the hill, and moved toward the pile of brush that had burned up with most of their gas. The fire was out, though, and the embers soaked. He turned and walked toward Pete but stopped for some reason and stepped back, as if he saw something in Pete's face that frightened him. Pete had never seen Jack misstep in the woods, but he watched now as Jack slipped on a patch of ice and hit the ground, snapping his leg against a rock. Jack made his hands into fists and held them in front of his chest. His jaw clenched and his eyes clamped shut. It was sleeting more than raining now, the temperature dropping fast. They were soaked to the skin.

"The coats, our clothes?" Jack asked but then seemed to remember.

Pete tried to picture how far it was to the intersection where Doug had gone for gas. A few miles. It wasn't far, Pete told himself. He was hazy from hours of the saw buzzing through his thoughts, and he couldn't decide if they were really in danger or not. The sun had just been out, and it was only sleet and rain. It was almost spring, not the middle of the winter, but they might be more than a few miles from the intersection.

Jack rolled over on his side. Dirt and sawdust funneled into the creases around his eyes and mouth.

"It's twisted. You walk it," Jack said. "Down to the store at the crossing."

"I can't leave you here," Pete said.

"You got to. We wasted too much time already."

The wind had swung around to the north and picked up force. On the way down the hill, Pete slipped and fell but pulled himself up by a branch. It had been an easy climb up earlier, but now he had to lower himself from tree to tree across a field of ice. It seemed to take forever, and when he reached the road, it was impossible to get his footing on the glassy surface. Maybe someone would come along, he thought, but this was a logging road and the paper company wasn't cutting in this area anymore. There was no reason to come down this way.

He lunged forward into a sluggish jog, his joints stiff, his whole body shaking, his arms dead weight. He couldn't understand how he had gotten so cold so fast, and he slipped again, the road rising up like a fist and smacking him in the side of the head. The gray sky whirled and the ground pitched. He felt as drunk as he had been on the night of the accident, when Jen helped him out of the party and into the passenger seat. She had been drinking, too, but not as much. He passed out and didn't wake up until the car was in a spin, and he curled his arms over his head just before he shot through the front windshield and landed in the grass. Both his arms were broken in several places, and his neck hurt. After a few minutes, he managed to roll onto his knees and stand, still drunk, to walk over to the car. The wet road shimmered in the glow of the one remaining headlight. Jen leaned against the steering wheel, her face torn and smashed. She was still breathing, he could tell, from the bubbles in the blood around her busted nose. When the police found him, he was down the road stumbling away with his broken arms flopping at his sides. Later, when they asked why he had run, he said he was going for help, but after a while, he was no longer sure. He might just have been running.

He had no idea how long he had been on the ground by the time he pushed himself back up to his knees. He was afraid of the ground's claim on him. In another hour, maybe less, it would be dark and even colder. His legs sliced forward in slow motion. In fits and starts, he managed a jog for a few minutes only to tumble down again. Panic thrummed in his chest. He wasn't far away from people, but he might as well be in the middle of the north woods. The skin of his arms was pale around the scars from the injuries.

When he finally made it up to his feet once more, he couldn't be sure which direction led to the store. The shape of the woods didn't help, the ice on the road showed no sign of his passing. The sleet pelted his eye-lids. A white boulder looked familiar. He must have passed it already, but maybe when they first drove in. He took a step back from the boulder, which seemed to grow paler in the dimming light, and his arms and legs and shoulders broke into such a feverish shiver that the boulder shook out of his vision.

He needed a rest, and he sat down and covered his face with his hands. The heat of a sob wouldn't come to his eyes, as it hadn't since he could remember; he bared his teeth, let out a low growl and then lay down on the side of the road to lean his head on the ice. For Jen's parents, this would be final proof that everything he touched fell to pieces. No one would blame him for not getting up again. He stopped thinking and listened to the rain and sleet patter through the woods on either side of the road. The sound formed a blanket around his thoughts. He pictured Jen's mother hearing about his death. Her eyes would close and her upper lip would curl. She would shake her head. "Well," she would say, nothing more, not a note of pity in her voice. He had stayed away from Jen since the accident, not because of the injuries to her face, as she and everyone else probably thought, but because he had started to believe what her parents said about him.

Pete closed his eyes, and in the white shadow flickering across the backs of his eyelids, he saw Jack's pale cheeks, as delicate as old linens. Days after Pete had moved back into his parents' house, his arms still in casts, Jack showed up at the front door. No one had asked him to come.

"You ever been to one of these?" Jack asked in the truck. Pete said no, and Jack shrugged. "Here's how it goes: everybody says they're an alcoholic, no one really thinks they are."

Jack showed up again two days later. Even after they started working together, he showed up every other evening at six-thirty. On the trips to and from the meetings, Jack remained silent and hunched over the steering wheel like a cab driver getting paid by the mile. Once, on the way home, Pete complained about someone in the meeting who had gone on too long, and Jack replied, "Ahhh, you're just a spoiled punk." Pete slammed the door when he got out of the truck and thought that was it between them, but Jack was there to pick him up for work the next morning and there again for the meeting that night. Going to meetings with Jack, even after he drank, and later working for him, was an obligation Pete had wanted to escape from the start, and he suspected Jack had wanted to escape it as well. He had no idea, looking back, how it had become an obligation, but that's what it was.

He got to his feet. The shaking stopped and he thought maybe he was warming up, but his hair and arms were covered with ice. He had taken his T-shirt off again but didn't remember doing so.

He made it around a curve in the road, and saw in the distance the store and gas station. His knees would hardly bend, and though he tried to keep the store in sight, he had to look down, too, in order not to slip.

The store was closed, the windows dark. There were no cars in the lot, but a door slammed nearby and just down the road a guy stepped out of his truck and walked into a ramshackle bar with a neon Bud sign hanging in the window. Pete went to the door of the bar, but he couldn't turn the knob—his hands wouldn't grip hard enough—and his voice wouldn't work. He was feet away from getting warm but had no way inside. He swung his arm from the shoulder and tried to pound on the door, but he could only manage to tap the surface. Desperate, he fell to his knees and collapsed with his back against the door. He could hear the beat of music from inside the bar.

Pete closed his eyes and pictured a cold gray afternoon in March five years ago when his father had decided to go out behind their house and chop more firewood, which he had ordered late so it was unsplit and green. His father set his ninth beer of the afternoon on the hood of the car and pulled the light axe out of the splitting log where it had been rusting since the fall. He muscled a three-foot-wide piece of maple off the pile, rolled it flat onto the soggy ground, raised the axe high above his head and slipped on a patch of ice, falling to one knee. The second time he raised the axe above his head, he splayed his legs for balance and brought the axe down squarely on the log. The blade sank in only a few inches; the axe was too light. He needed a maul, but even that might not be enough when the wood was green. His father placed his foot on top of the log and tugged on the axe handle until the blade popped out. After half an hour of watching his father work on the same log, Pete couldn't stand it any more, and he went upstairs. But even with his face buried in the mattress and the pillow clamped over his head, Pete still heard the thud of the axe. It seemed as if the thudding had always been there, as relentless as the ticking of a clock (he could hear it now as he banged the back of his head against the door to the bar). He let his chin fall against his chest and he squeezed his eyes shut, but the banging continued in his thoughts: the rusted axe head rising over his father's head and crashing back down into the green wood again and again.

If Jack were not waiting for him on top of the hill, Pete never would have opened his eyes. There was Jack's truck parked just a few feet in front of his outstretched legs. He crawled to the driver's side and pushed himself to his feet by leaning against the cab. The window was caked with ice, but he could see the keys in the ignition. A flash of heat passed through his thoughts: his heart raced and he could taste metal. His hands were half closed and his fingers wouldn't uncurl, but he hooked his fingertips on the latch and yanked up until the door popped open enough for him to nudge in and pull it shut. He leaned his head against the steering wheel and pressed his knuckles together around the keys. He tried to twist, but he couldn't feel his fingers and the keys kept slipping out of his grip. It was dark again; he had closed his eyes. His hands dropped to his sides, and he heard the whine of a dog hungry for its dinner coming from his own chest.

He woke some time later with a terrible ache in his limbs. The engine was on and the heater blasting, though he didn't remember getting the keys to twist. It hurt to close his hands, but he worked them loose and managed to pull the truck onto the road. He had to drive slowly on the translucent ice as blankets of rain and sleet washed over the cab. Nothing looked familiar between passes of the wipers until he saw a large maple. Their footprints had been washed away, but he recognized the spot, and as he tugged on his dry shirt and pants in the cab, the rain and sleet eased off to a drizzle. With a bundle of clothes tucked under his arm, he struggled up the hill. He had to pull himself from tree to tree over the ice. His joints were so swollen and stiff that he moved sluggishly, as if through water.

When he reached the top of the hill, he looked around, but Jack wasn't there. Pete yelled his name, his voice hoarse and cracking like a boy's. Fresh tree limbs had been pulled into a mound over the ashes of the brush Doug had burned, and Pete peeled them off like scales until he found the charred core of what looked at first like a bundle of blackened sticks. A pair of eyes flashed from the middle of the pile, wide white globes centered with green and black. They vanished and appeared again. Gradually, Pete distinguished Jack's body curled naked with his knees pulled up to his chest and every inch of his skin and hair caked with a thick layer of ash and mud. Jack opened his mouth slowly and his pink tongue appeared. Maybe he was about to speak, but no words came out. He seemed half his normal size. Pete leaned down and draped a coat over him.

"We have to go," Pete said, but Jack just stared blankly at him as if he no longer understood the language.

"Not leaving," Jack said, his voice barely audible. He reached out to push the coat away. "I'm waiting for Doug."

The light completely failed, and Pete only knew Jack was still there by touching Jack's arms, which were as cold as blocks of wood. Pete reached under the crusted torso and tried to lift, but Jack had seized his arms around a granite boulder and couldn't or wouldn't let go. Even as Jack's breathing slowly eased to a trickle, he still clung to the rock. Pete couldn't pull him up.

"Jack, we have to go—I can't leave you here," Pete said.

"No," Jack said. "I'm staying."

Jack closed his eyes, and Pete spread his arms and legs over Jack, making himself into a blanket.

"It's me," Pete said into Jack's ear. "It's Doug." His face stung under the wet streams pouring over his cheeks. "I'm sorry," he said. His voice echoing through the dark woods even sounded like Doug's, and for a moment he felt as if he were Jack's son returning to offer forgiveness and to be forgiven.

Jack let go of the boulder, and Pete pulled him up. Together they slid from tree to tree down the hill, and when they reached the pavement, Pete cradled Jack in his arms and carried him the rest of the way.

The cab was warm, and Pete piled dry clothes over Jack, aiming the heater vents at his face. Pete called Jack's name as he hit the gas and after there was no answer, he reached out and touched the side of Jack's cold face. "Wake up!" he yelled and drove as if it wasn't too late, speeding down the icy road with the back wheels fishtailing in and out of ruts. After they passed through the intersection and a few miles later joined the main road back to Vaughn, Jack opened his eyes and leaned over the dash to stare at the path the high beams cut through the night.

RIVER RUNNER

1976. The last pulp drive down the Kennebec and there were no alewives in dark schools waiting to ascend the falls, no shad or striped bass or blueback herring. Nothing in the river but sinkers and bark cake and raw waste from sixteen towns coating the bottom, methane bubbling up through the water and pulp in the booms waiting for a freshet.

Harry Clough put in upriver from the head of the drive so he wouldn't have to deal with the new drive boss, Gerald Young, some hard hat from Scott who'd never set foot on a log. His bateau drifted, needing no encouragement, and the river gradually took on the shape he remembered. The water brushed along a low bank of thick bayberry and alder and wildflowers. Many a man lost his footing and with not a moment to glance at the others ashore or at the pile man or at the pole man in the bateau holding upriver, he was swept under and maybe never seen, maybe pinched between two sinkers and dragged to the bottom. It's part of the reason the river still ran so brown.

When he spotted the hippie director in charge of a documentary film crew getting misinformation from Gerald Young on shore, Harry gave them all the finger. Gerald Young waved him in, and yelled that Harry was going to get himself killed.

"I ain't gonna bear-hug no dry kye out of the alder swamps," Harry yelled. He hadn't greased up his three-and-sixty case-hardened nail-caulked boots to tromp through the mud. Harry'd show them what it was like to run over a thousand feet of race to escape the better part of a fallen forest bearing down.

"You're Haywire Harry, aren't you," one of the crew yelled from shore. "You're the one who rode a log though the sluice at Thirteen Mile Woods in that movie back in '49."

So what? Maybe he was. Man in the suit had paid him five bucks, paid him five bucks to do it again.

Harry drifted out of view and followed the course of the current for three-quarters of an hour, until he spotted the farm that belonged to his old friend, Johnny Jardine, who stood down on the bank of the river at the end of his hay field. The water slackened over a shallow bar of stones and the bateau bottomed out. A jam behind him already. What a goddamned jackpot, what a bunch of bank beavers, the so-called rivermen in charge of this operation. He paddled over to the bank and jumped over the side into the cold water. Right away the midges and blackflies were on him.

"They rimracked the country, ain't they Harry?" Johnny yelled from up high on the bank. "I didn't think I'd see you out here."

Harry visited Johnny once a year during the drive. They had spent more than a few winters together north of the Dead. Between the two of them, nothing but the forest for a coat. Frozen ants falling out of the bark tasted like cranberries. Bunk down next to the horses to get rid of the lice. Wake up smelling of manure. Johnny seemed older than he had last year. He hunched over and leaned on a stick. Gravity pulled at his jowls and shoulders and wrists. A young man, the son or the grandson, stood next to him, the spit image of the Johnny that Harry remembered. Harry and Johnny were about the same age, but Harry didn't think of himself as this age. This broken man.

"Haven't seen you in years now," Johnny said, and Harry stared at him, confused. "Look there. The boys'll have a terrible job. The logs're ricked up just like Rose's jackstraws."

Other guys on the bank squinted at Harry as he made his way out of the water.

"I gotta git down the river," Harry said. "Wife's gonna have another baby."

"Member we used to say to her down in Vaughn come winter: 'We don't like the climate down south, time to head north.' She'd say, 'the climate of any place where you have regular work never did and never will suit you.' She's right there. I've rid logs down the b'il-in'est rapids of the Kennebec and never lost my head, but coming home in the spring after the drive was unsettlin'."

Harry handed over the whiskey, and they both took a snort.

"What's an old man like you doing snigging logs out of the woods?" Johnny said and looked out over the river at the four-foot pulp nosing around the boulders. "The boards that the old trees made—no wain, no knots, no bark showing, nothing under eight inches. Look at this wood—there's nothing else left. Skunk spruce. That's something, I can't understand it, ruina-tion."

Harry said, "I'm having a baby."

"You're having a baby." Johnny stepped back and leaned against a tree. His grandson or son—whatever he was—gripped his arm but otherwise kept staring into space, like a man holding a leash while his dog pissed.

"She's waiting on me now. I gotta go," Harry said and climbed down the bank.

Johnny laughed so hard he dropped his stick and had to lean on the arm of the kid, his head arched back, mouth open, laughing. No front teeth. A row of other guys standing on the bank laughed, too.

"Hey Harry," someone yelled from shore. "Did you really kill a guy in the woods with your caulked boots?"

Harry looked up at the boys—different boys, different faces than he remembered, but the same boys. All this time and that's all they remembered. Harry was twenty-three when that story started, and he wasn't about to answer to it again. He climbed into his bateau and pushed off. The small wooden boat mixed in with the pulpwood and moved sideways downriver.

"Is it true?" Melinda had asked years before when the story reached her of how he had gone into the woods with the PEI boy to fell trees and come back to camp alone.

"I came back alone, but I didn't do nothing to him," he said. No one had believed him. They were cutting on the edge of a swamp in the middle of winter, he and the PEI boy pulling on the saw. Harry looked up as the giant spruce groaned and smashed down through the forest in front of him. The PEI boy had been standing behind him, but when Harry turned around, no one was there. The saw lay in the snow next to the man's kennebeker and his spare socks and the kilhig pole they used to push the trees in the right direction. The rest of the camp searched the area just before dark. They twitched out the last tree Harry had felled and even some of the other sticks. They tried to dig around in the snow down to the duff, but it was as deep in some places as a man standing. You sure hid him good, someone said, and they gave up. There was no more time to search, with thousands of cords to cut before the drive in the spring.

It was a dawn cup of boiling tea then. Biscuits, bean hole beans. Lugging the bateau over blowdowns and gullies and cradle knolls, through shallow water, always downriver. Someone would yell, Harry, your nose is freezing and you'd rub snow on it until the pain came back. Feet always wet, stubs, and always the peaveys, the long polls with the iron spike and the swinging iron hook that would clamp a log. The peavey would not let go, if you had log sense: tendencies of currents, effects of different volumes of water, places where jams formed, and the reason for them, key-log methods, and rollway breaking, and dam running. Moving the logs, and keeping out of the water when you could. An extra pair of socks better than almighty faith. Shallow water was fine, just get wet, but deep water swallowed men down.

For years, running for Dan Bosse, Harry was the man to shoot a jam: out over the logs and find the key log in against a boulder, set the dynamite stick in and light the fuse, start running. Wait for the crash, the water spouting straight up in the air, and finally the rush forward—step on a lead log and sweep downriver. Dog the peavey into another log and wait until you hit the current. Then the log settled right down. You could ride it out.

Unless you weren't lucky. There was a kid, Hutchinson, in '38 on Pollywog went under for twenty rods, but the water flung him up onto a granite shelf and he stood there unhurt, shaking his head, water pouring out of his mouth. Vernon was watching from a jill-poke log and as soon as Hutchinson popped out, Vernon's log was swept away and later they found him downriver. A death call across the long swamp that night. Buried his body in a cask. Hung his boots from a tree. No one touched those boots, no one cut that tree. They rotted off the tree, or the tree rotted under them.

Tonight he was going to sleep in his own bed. Melinda would be standing on the porch in her apron, in sight of both the river and the kitchen, where there was sure to be something other than beans and cakes and tea on the stove. He would toss his pannikin in the barn for the season, and eat off real plates, sleep in a real bed, no rollout in the morning. The warm skin at the nape of her neck.

People standing on the banks waved to him, and he waved back with his peavey. Song like a hard rain through summer maples caught his ear—the pulpwood coming down—and inside this sound he had come to dread and wait on since he was sixteen was the call of someone's voice. And not just someone but a woman, and not just a woman but Mrs. Clough, Melinda Clough, his wife, calling for him to hurry home. Harry looked downriver, thinking of Melinda strutting across the field behind their house just before he left for the drive yelling, "Harry Clough, I want a word with you." As if he were one of their children. And it was never one word. Never.

It started to rain, but Melinda wouldn't get wet waiting on the bank in Vaughn. She had the trick, always did, of stepping between his thoughts.

A heavy-duty outboard, a company boat, came up from behind. Not the hippie film crew but a bunch of hard hats.

"You all right there old man?" A fat kid yelled from the helm. Two others stood behind him with big grins. "You got rough water up ahead, you know."

Some fink of a company man on the Machias once said to him: "Harry, you're through, you're a shit disturber." Harry flew through the air feet first and thunked his spiked boots into the man's chest. A little logger's smallpox to remember him by. He could see himself doing the same thing now, but his legs would no more obey his thoughts than the river.

"I wasn't brought up to wear the seat of my pants out," he yelled, but it didn't come out right. He sounded weak.

"Old man, the boss sent us up to get you outta the way. He wants you in the rear."

"I already told him I ain't picking the rear, and I have to get downriver—wife's having a baby. I gotta get back in time." The end of his sentence trailed off. He couldn't be sure now what he was saying. The guys in the boat laughed, but not as much as the previous group of guys, and he wanted to kill them for not laughing enough, or for laughing at all.

"That's funny, old man, but we're serious," one of them said.

The boat pulled up alongside and one of the kids reached forward with a rope to tie onto the bateau. Harry swung the point of his peavey down onto the gunnels right between the kid's fingers.

"Christ!"

Another grabbed onto Harry by the shoulder and pulled him half over into the outboard. Harry smacked the kid in the jaw with the handle of his peavey. The one driving the boat lunged for him, and Harry dodged and swung a full circle with the peavey's iron hook gaping like a bear jaw. They all ducked as the weight of the peavey carried Harry off his feet into the bow of the bateau where his arm cracked against the seat, and he smacked his jaw on the bottom.

The driver of the launch gunned them a safe distance away as Harry pulled himself to his feet.

"I ain't going upriver!" he shouted. He had to go downriver. He had no choice; he was already late.

"Have it your way, old man."

Their engine roared back. The wrong Christly way. Like to see those kids at Garfield Falls, where the river dropped forty, fifty feet, and the logs piled up at the bottom, cribbed right into the woods, and it was a job someone *had to do*. That's what he would tell those kids. It was a job someone had to do, and that meant someone was going do it. That someone was Dan Bosse or Harry, someone who had been chucked on the side of the road when he was sixteen, married when he was seventeen, a father at eighteen, going through life loaded for bears. Someone had to lower down on a rope into Garfield Falls. Melinda would say let someone else, but if someone had to go, there was no choice for any of them, was there? On a rope to the bottom of Garfield Falls with an axe, forty feet below the crib-work of logs, he chopped one handed at the key log until it snapped and the whole forest came down, logs whipping by inches in front of his face as the boys pulled him up through the cascade.

It wasn't just that there was no one else to do it. She didn't understand. It was what he did. You wouldn't end up in a cask, would you, not if you were good, if you were quick, if you were lucky. The time three of them stood on top of the sluice at Upper Dam when a sixteen-foot log popped and shot at them sideways like a missile, someone whistled and all three jumped three feet straight up in the air one after another, landing again one, two, three after the log had passed under.

The peavey in Harry's left hand dropped into the bottom of the boat. His hand wouldn't open or close. He picked the peavey up with his right hand and leaned on it. The pain was nothing but a tight vibration along his collar, but the worst was coming. In a fight yesterday or years ago (or was it an accident?), Danny Sumner drove the iron point of his peavey right through the soft part of Harry's foot, pinning him to a log up by Twenty-Six Islands. The name was right, anyway, and the place. It had happened.

"You all right?" Dan Bosse said.

"Don't feel a thing," Harry said, looking down at his foot pinned to the log. Nothing more true. Nine hours in the river, walking on dead man's legs. "Let the gutters run with whiskey, boys."

Pulled out the iron spike, dried his foot, and poured Dan's rum over the hole. Like a vacation until it thawed.

Now he could hear the white water up ahead, and for the first time in his life on a river he didn't know where he was. The easy bend, the gray humped-back hills to the south. Fields came right down to the river, and the pulp moved forward in the churning current at the same pace as the bateau. He didn't even know where they sent this short poke: Anson, North Anson, Norridgewock? The names of places—the sounds in his mouth—didn't match the images flipping through his head; the Nezinscott, the Webb above Berry Mills. Alder stream into the Dead or Sandy stream into the Carrabasset into Gilman stream, Misery River, Martin stream—all flowing into the Kennebec. Weir Falls, Sorrow Falls, Island Falls. All flowing into the Kennebec. The Kennebec, he was on the Kennebec, or flowing into it. Because that's where he lived, where he was going: raspberries, and along the stone walls, wild currants, gooseberries, the first Pippins, Summer

Sweetings. Running barefoot along the cow path of his grandfather's place in New Portland. Stewed beans and biscuits or fried pork and potatoes. You could smell it cooking from the brook.

He steadied himself in the bateau and looked up to see a girl running through the field along the shore. She held her skirt in one hand and waved to him with the other. Her father walked behind her, loping with his hands in his pockets, hat tilted back on his head.

Melinda had said "I want to have a word with you," and he turned around like a schoolboy. *But you might as well wish for the day of his death/For he'll drink rum as long as he draws his breath*—that song the boys sang. Only the boys in camp knew what it was like, dying to get away from home and dying to get back.

The white water appeared in a line across the river along with a rising grumble creeping back along the banks and through the grass. He had no bowman, no paddle to shoot the rapids. The girl in the field ran and ran, jumping over stones and reaching higher with her arm, waving to him. Her father yelled for her to slow down and be careful. Harry waved back, lifting his peavey into the air, and he remembered a day like this one, cold and sharp, when a solid jam built up right across the river above the falls, ice coming over the top and plowing into the woods, driving logs through trees. Old Danny ran out with dynamite and waited on the jam to make sure. The blast sent him ten feet in the air and back down with two boots steady on the same log.

They made for out and she broke. Harry stepped and for the first time ever there was nothing there. He fell deep, buried in black water under a raft of birling logs. He could reach up and touch them, but the water was so cold his hands were already numb and there was no light shining through. He scratched at the bark and pounded the eighteen-inch stumps with his fists, but he might as well have been trying to dig his way out of a grave. His limbs went slack, he stopped fighting, and he opened his eyes on darkness.

The current swept him faster than the logs and shot him straight out over the falls thirty feet down through the crystal air. He sank into the pool below and knew enough to hold his breath and stay down and push his way until he grounded out. He started drinking on the ride into Portland where he bought a new suit and got a room and stayed drunk three days until he surfaced penniless and bruised to a pulp and remembered he was supposed to be home. That had been his last thought before falling through the gap between those logs: Melinda is waiting, she's due any day now. A baby. He was still drunk by the time he hitched home, and she yelled at him until he went out to the barn for another bottle, which he kept beneath the hay in one of the empty stalls where the dog now slept. He was supposed to bring his pay home this time. Before he left she had said, "I want to have a word with you. A word. For once, we need that pay here, Harry."

She screamed at him in the rain while he marched right by her into the house where the stove blasted in the kitchen. His son, the youngest, and the two daughters, wasting his firewood. He cut it, he split it. Melinda right behind him. The kitchen was no bigger than a man's grave. He whipped around, just trying to thrash his way out, just trying to come up for air, and suddenly she was on the floor where he had thrown her against the wall, blood gushing out from between her legs. The smell of it, the taste of metal. No phone then. He stumbled out into the field, trying to run for help, but his legs gave out and on his knees in the rain he began to turn as numb as he had to the spike of the peavey driven through his foot. When his oldest daughter arrived at his side, all he could do was point down the valley toward town. She started running across the field, between the old apple trees grown wild, and along the trail that followed the river. Lighting flashed once on her pale arms churning through the rain. She ran but not fast enough for the baby, not fast enough to keep Melinda and the rest of them from dying to him. He never spoke to any of them again. Melinda made sure of that.

Harry sat down in the bateau and rested the peavey on his lap. On the riverbank, the girl stopped running as her father called for her to come back, and she waved to Harry one last time before turning to her father, who leaned against the fence looking across the water. Her skirt fanned out around her knees, and with each leap forward she seemed about to sail into the sky.

LIFE DURING PEACETIME

I can tell by the way she stands that my mother wants
me to ride the bike she bought for my birthday. It is a
shame to think of a new bike rusting against the side of
the carriage house, so I sit on the seat and coast down
the slope of the driveway toward her. At one point, I
can't remember when, I learned how to balance in
motion.

I have other toys—a kite, plastic cars—that she
bought. For some reason, handing things to me is dis-
tasteful to her, so she usually leaves them in my room
or outside the back door for me to find. If she is standing in the window or sitting in one of the chairs looking down over the river, I will sometimes push a toy car
along the granite slab that once served as the foundation for the small barn before it burned down. I have
no way of knowing if she derives any satisfaction from
seeing me do such things, or if she sees me at all.

I am supposed to start fourth grade in the fall, going
to school for the first time, but I already know what it

will be like to wait in line by the drinking fountain for Mrs. Nason to signal it is time to walk down the hall toward the lunchroom. I already hate the smell of steam rising off the asphalt playground after a thunderstorm and the dry smell of chalk in the damp classroom and the antiseptic smell of the boys' bathroom. My mother has given me books at home until now and I don't see why anything has to change, but she says I have to go—everyone has to at some point—even though she worries my father might come home while I'm away. I might miss him.

He's not coming home, I say when I ride past her.

We have this argument every morning. I am convinced that he's dead to us, while she thinks he is making his slow way back to us in the only way he can, because he wants, as we all do, for things to go back to the way they were before the war.

It's all right, I tell her, stepping off my bike. Let's go wind the clocks.

It has been a tradition since the Revolution for every generation who lives in this house to leave behind a clock, and, while my father sits in his office downtown, it is my mother's job to wind them, a job she dutifully carries out once a week before the mechanism springs expire. It's not hard to wind the clocks, and some day the job will be mine. For now, I hold open the doors as she inserts the keys, and for a while afterward, we sit together on the green couch listening to the knocks and clicks in the hollow boxes.

The coil at the center of my father's purpose unwound one afternoon and for him the ticking stopped. When the war came, he didn't sign up, as his father had done and his father's father had done, and so on. During one of the Sunday dinners we used to have together when my grandmother was still alive, my father told my grandfather that he wasn't going to go. My grandfather stood up from the table and said, I don't have a son. And he walked back across the road to the old dairy farm where he lives. In the Second World War, he carried with him in his tank as he crossed France the cavalry pistol his father had carried through the same country on horseback. He remembers those days as if they were yesterday, but he can't remember yesterday. I often hear him nailing one board to another for no reason. He inspects the milking machines after the hired man has already inspected them.

My father lives in his office on Water Street and has been living there since he did not sign up for the war. At night he lies flat with his arms at his sides and his mouth hanging open, the portrait of a man sleeping. When he speaks to himself, his voice is a trickle. During the day, when people knock on his door, as they rarely do anymore, he sits there in a plastic chair with his windbreaker in his lap, as quiet as an empty glass of water. He sits behind his name written in gold lettering across the wide pane of glass, behind the oak

203

desk, behind the three pens, the blotter, the phone, the brass lamp.

My father was born with exceptionally long flat feet and cannot walk more than a mile without having to sit down. He has to have special shoes made by a cobbler in Augusta. He is allergic to wool. Even if he had been drafted, they would have sent him home. At six-five, he is an enormous man, but when he sits, he hunches and his narrow limbs collapse inward like wings. It's difficult to see him in his office at first, but he's in there. He was exhausted by the fighting long before the war started, before I was born, and before he married a woman from a good family, my mother, and moved her back to the river town where he was born.

A woman named Janet Robinson thinks she looked in the window of his office last year (when helicopters were lifting people off the roof of the Saigon embassy on the front page of the *Valley Journal*) and saw him sitting behind his desk with tears washing down the slope of his face. She knocked on the door, she said, but he did not move. She mistook sadness for the reflection of the river in the glass, and mistook the man she saw inside for my father (he had the same reaching nose and anvil face), just as my mother has begun to mistake the man in her memory for the men in the portraits on the walls of our house. In her memory, he speaks, he sips his coffee, but she is not sure now if she can remember a word he has ever said.

Mrs. Small saw him on Water Street early one morning when she got up to walk the dog. At four in the morning, he drives his rusty Chevrolet to Augusta to buy milk and cheese at an all-night convenience store.

I am told that before I was born he would spend hours walking through the acreage, lying down when he felt like it and letting his arms sink into the wood sorrel and bluets. My grandfather has called him a dreamer. A man who has lost his way. His hair, Mrs. Small said, was down to his shoulders when she saw him. Janet Robinson thinks she heard music coming from the back room of his office. She could barely hear it, she said. She had to press her ear to the glass; for some reason she also thinks my father is carving pieces of wood back there, and he may be. Wood shavings pile up behind the building.

After I help my mother with the clocks, I go to the upper field where my father talks to me as if he were there. He travels in his thoughts to Montana or California or Idaho as he talks to me, revealing the most banal details of the things he saw the summer before he met my mother. I tell him I would like to see Nebraska as he has seen it, and roll my eyes over the great central plain, but he doesn't respond. At the end of our conversation, during which he has not listened to a word I have said (even though I shout over his voice), he reminds me that he has not been here to visit, and that we have not had a conversation. The house, the land, and all its history belong to you, he says. He calls me the child king, and then says good-bye.

My mother pretends he is on his way home, and I pretend he visits me in the upper field.

My last name is the name of the town where we live. The king granted us this land at a time when our schooners crowded the docks along the banks of the Kennebec to haul hundred-foot pines, granite, and ice to England, Hong Kong, and Calcutta. The docks have rotted into the mud, the windows of our shoe factory are boarded up, the roads are cracked, and the clap-boards of the old federals are soft to the touch. The last of our wealth is in the land, six hundred acres, part of which we let to a local farmer for the cost of groceries and part of which we open to the public as a park for a break on taxes so that it can remain ours, if in name only, and so that it might, when I have reached the pro-prietary age, become mine until the next generation when it will be someone else's job to wind the clocks. But none of this may come to pass. It's possible that no one will grow older here.

My mother goes into the old study where the photo-graphs are strewn over the floor. Though as a boy my father looked much the way I do now, I have held his photo while looking at myself in the beveled mirror and there is no way I can reproduce the smile he wears sitting on top of the five-foot wheel of the tractor. It makes me think I was never his age.

She spreads the photos out, the ones of my father when he was young mixed with the ones she took of him when they first met. She picks them up, holds them close to her face, and puts them down. There were pictures of her, too, when she was twenty, but she has picked those out over time and burned them in the fireplace, presumably for the same reason she never looks in the mirror. Even when I stand in front of her and ask a question, she doesn't look me in the eye.

She's pulled other photo albums out of the trunk, of my grandfather's days after the war when he first met my grandmother, and they drove around town in their Packard and took the Woolwich down the Kennebec to Bath. My father was not supposed to be an only child, but my grandfather had an affair with a woman in Augusta when he was serving in the state legislature, and my grandmother found out about it. She didn't talk to him for a whole year, even though they lived in the same house, and they never slept in the same bed again. I was an accident (at the beginning of the war), but I suppose that I wasn't meant to be an only child, either.

There are photos of my grandmother (the surfaces peel off like fly wings), and a tin photo of my great-grandfather sitting in a chair on the lawn (which has since overgrown with thistle and bayberry) just after he returned from the war. He sits in the chair as if in the saddle of a horse, his beard covering all but his stolid eyes. I often carry the tin type around in my pocket. If I turn it in the direct light, the image disappears. I carry several photos with me—I don't know why—and occasionally I exchange the ones I have for others in the pile, depending on how I feel. Maybe I carry them because there are no photos of me anywhere in the house. I do worry that I might not be here at all.

My favorite picture is of my father when he was younger than I am now, sitting in a wicker chair with his eyes peacefully closed and his legs crossed and hands folded in his lap like an old man.

My mother turns and says I should stop sneaking up behind her, to act my age, and busy myself with the toys she has bought for me. She covers up what she has been doing, as if embarrassed, goes downstairs to put a record on the phonograph, and sits in a wicker chair leaned up against the edge of the house near the open window. She falls asleep by the time the record finishes and doesn't hear the needle scratching over the middle of the disc. The sound reminds me of certain moments in old movies when an actor enters a room where someone they love has died.

I stand over her while she sleeps and ask her to stop waiting for my father, but she often stays up all night reading a novel and can't be woken until the afternoon. Someone has to be awake in case he does come home, so I run outside to drag a branch along the jagged surface of the old stone wall, clicking off the seconds and holding my breath when I see barbed wire passing right through the middle of a tree trunk. It's bad luck otherwise.

I hear a car braking down the road, and the voices of kids from town passing through the leaves, but I see no one except the man now climbing to the upper field, a very fat man who used to be mayor before I was born. He ambles up the slope each day at this time, stopping every five or six steps to breathe. After a few minutes standing in the middle of the field, looking down the hill to the sluice and below that to the stream, he lies down and rests the back of his hand over his eyes. The starlings seem drunk in the grass. The yarrow and aster are past their bloom and the thrush's flute, so welcome a month ago, has started to strain. I think I can hear the webbed feet of the ducks pushing through the current of the river below the lower field.

My mother comes outside and rubs her eyes, looking into the old pool, which has been dry and cracked since long before I was born. Speaking softly, as if to herself, she says my name and that she wants to go for a drive. I have been no farther north than the Schoodic Peninsula and no farther south than Kittery Point, both times with my mother in our light-blue sedan. The air has cleared and cooled by the time she pulls out of the barn. She has not wanted to drive much this summer; I had almost forgotten the feeling of the trees whipping by and the sudden hard glances of the people in town whom we rarely see.

As she puts the car in gear and coasts toward Water Street, I hold my hand out the window and pretend we are flying on the wing of my fingers. At moments like these, I am conscious of being happy, and I turn to her to ask if she is happy. This is a game we used to play, and she flinches and looks out the window, trying to make me think she doesn't want me to go on, though I know she does. "You are happy, Mother," I say, and she pretends not to hear as we cross the Augusta Bridge, suspended seventy feet up, in midair. "You are so, so happy, Mother," I say again, and she breaks out in tears, though she smiles as she wipes her face.

On the way back, she pulls off the road across the river from our town and looks out over the water.

"It's as if I've always lived here," she says.

"We can leave," I say.

But she is afraid that if we drive down the road any farther (in the direction of the city and the state where she was born), we will travel forever forward in a straight line until even this moment is forgotten. She turns right across the river and climbs the hill back to the house.

I wish we had kept driving. I don't say anything. She is sad enough without the burden of my disappointment.

We go over to sit with my grandfather while he drinks his afternoon tea, and he talks to us about Patton's rush to Berlin and the German girl he met in Freiburg and almost married, as if we have never heard these stories before. He tells my mother that she is as beautiful as the day she first came to town. Then he puts his hand on my shoulder and leaves it there while he turns to me with hazy eyes. His skin smells of pipe smoke as he pulls me over. His hands are bent and spotted and dirty. Even though he is almost blind, he is the only one who sees me, so I have to believe what he says. We live in two worlds, he says. The one we fight for, and the one we fight against. And he starts in on all the people he thinks are ruining this town. After so many years, he has quite a list, and I know all the names: the Dawsons, who own the store and over-charge and no longer make their own bread; Willoughby, the tax assessor just down the road; the Nasons; Mrs. Molloy; the MacDonalds, both of them; and so on. Someone wants to build a new school, someone lets their kids chase his cows through the field, someone's father said to my grandfather in a town meeting thirty-five years ago that he was a fool.

As my mother and I walk back across the road, I think that someday, if I am fortunate, I will have a few friends and sometimes, coming home with them after school, will think of myself as one of them. But even then as I walk along, led down the slope of the valley by the dark chimneys against the metal sky, it will be impossible not to remember this time, standing above the house with my fingertips resting on the high grass as I look up and see a single-engine plane bank over the river, disappear in the late afternoon glare, and reappear downriver, heading east toward Richmond. There is something in this moment, beyond the sight of the plane's white wings turning in the currents, that recalls a time I can't quite reach, leaving me with the sense that I have been here before.

I walk through the side door and pass the portraits in the dark stairwell leading up to the third floor, where discarded furniture is stored in the spare rooms, the spindles and legs cluttered together like piles of weapons from a defeated army. No one ever painted portraits of mothers, grandmothers, daughters or the boys who died young (no one will ever paint me), but we live here, too, in the contours of the buckling plaster.

My mother goes back to bed downstairs, and I sit in an armless rocking chair to wait for her to get up. I listen for the door in case I have to speak for her if someone knocks—I've learned to speak as adults do. Today I hear only the strange calls of the cicadas in the grass; my mother also hears them as she closes her eyes and pulls the frayed white sheet up around her neck. We wait so long for summer this far north that it seems to last forever when it arrives, bloating the air with the smell of wet mud at low tide. My mother is tired; I am tired, too, but I need to slow every moment of daylight against the coming dusk, when it will feel as though the river is everywhere all around me while what little I remember—the last year, the last two years—will expand to fill more than the history of my name in this town. Even now, there is still time left (after the heat has silenced the birds and if the train is not coming and if the river is at the turn of the tide and if the breeze is still) for it to be quiet before dark. I can hear my grand-father mowing the small lawn in front of his house with his rusty push mower, but then he stops, and the cicadas are silent.

When he forgets that I am listening and talks as if to himself, this is what my father tells me in the upper field: There's an old man who lives a mile down from the entrance to our property. He was in the war in Europe, but he was not a hero. He drove supplies to the front. Now he sits on a narrow patch of trimmed grass in a metal lawn chair and listens to his transistor radio. In the morning the sun beats down on his face and on the white face of his house. By midday, the angle of the light has passed over the peak of his roof and he goes inside. For forty years he was a stonecutter—a granite cutter. I think of him at least once a day. When the sun doesn't come out, he doesn't come out. He is no more aware of us than the clouds are aware of him. His body holds what he is thinking in the way the town holds all of us: with a kind of indifferent affection. I am like that man, my father says.

This is what I tell my father in the upper field: Jim Wally, the junior high reading teacher, and George Sumner, the high school guidance counselor, meet for a beer before dinner at the Wharf, across the street from my father's office. Both men are basketball coaches. They get together every week. The chief of police, Chuck Sheldon, joins them. His daughter plays for Jim Wally. They stare out at the river. Mr. Dawson stands in back of Dawson's Variety right now staring out at the river and having a cigarette. Across town, Mrs. Molloy shakes her head at her youngest son who has come home again with dirt on his hands. Show me your hands, she says to him, show me—but he won't take them out of his pockets. A mile west Missy wakes from a nap in her bed on what had been her grandfather's farm twenty years before. She feels sure she has woken to a noise, but as she sits there upright listening to the sun go down she hears nothing, neither her mother coming back from working at the hardware store, nor her father coming home from Bath Iron Works, nor her older brother back from his friend's house where they all drink beer.

It is high tide, it is supper time. Two boys three years older than me stand on a field at the edge of the school I will soon attend tossing a muddy baseball with frayed seams. The ball vanishes for a moment, soaring through a shadow, before slapping into one of their gloves.

I have tried hard not to believe in what I know is a boy's fantasy, nothing more, I tell my father in the upper field, and he solemnly nods. He knows that the war has spread like pollen through the neighborhood, over the valley and hills, sweeping us up in the flow of its course.

After dark, I climb into the attic and open my grand-father's GI trunk, pulling out his fatigues, rolling the cuffs, and tightening a string around my waist. The revolver he carried through the war used to feel as if it weighed more than me, but now it seems to get lighter every night.

I smear mud on my face before heading down the drive to look for the people my grandfather has accused over the years of ruining this town (they look like us, he has said, but they are not like us). Two streets away I slide along the side of a wall to a lighted window. A man in a plaid shirt, Larry Henry, a snowplow driver in winter and farmhand in summer, a man my grand-father has always accused of stealing apples from his orchard, stands over his sink. Each breath seems to exhale through my ears as I raise the pistol and pull back the trigger. Dozens of times over the last weeks I have killed this man, and each night he dies without knowing it. He keeps on, flawless in his method of scrubbing each plate, back and front, rinsing and dry-ing, as if there is no war, as if his life were not about to end. I shoot and after the click, I move on quickly, feel-ing the dying beat of his heart in my own chest.

The Molloys sit hunched over at the table in their kitchen in their house on Winthrop Street like people who have outlived their desires. They die without a word to each other, as they did last night and the night before. Kathy McDonald behind the half-canted blinds turns in her mirror before bed, turning her head with each revolution to meet herself. I shoot her as she pauses, captivated by her own stare, and move on to the next house on the street where I find the Dawsons sitting on opposite sides of a table looking into their drinks, whispering as if someone might overhear. I shoot them both and move on up the road, completing a grid, climbing the hood of a car to shoot one woman on the second floor, another man as he takes out the trash. It is hard to tell the enemy from the innocent in the dark where I can only see the outline of a face or a silhouette, and of course all these people will have to be killed again tomorrow night. It is not the kind of war anyone can win.

Tonight I take a different route home past my father's office. When he visits me in the upper field, my father makes me promise that I will not bother him down on Water Street. I can only visit you here in the upper field, he has said, if you promise not to interrupt my dream. So I promise, but I can no longer keep that promise. It is not the kind of war I can go on fighting alone.

In the reflection of the window of my father's office, I watch someone point a gun at me. Without warning, he shoots me, and I shoot him, but neither of us falls. I move as the reflection moves, bend as he bends, and, in one swift motion heave the pistol through the plate glass. The shatter tumbles down the empty street and echoes with the snap of a distant shot. When I pull away from the gaping hole, a small shard sticks in the top of my wrist, and a black trickle flows down between my knuckles.

My father, who has been waiting all this time for an attack, comes out of the back room to see glass spread over his desk and the blue metal of his grandfather's pistol lying on the floor. He recognizes the gun, even if he doesn't recognize me. His hands shake. He is dirty and unshaven. He can't remember how the fighting started anymore than I can, but he has been fighting all along, I can see, rising and falling and rising, without rest, behind the locked door of his office.

The days are peaceful here in Vaughn, I try to explain to my father, in case he has forgotten, but after the sun falls over the western hill, all the people we have known in the daylight fight against us. I would gladly think otherwise, I say to him, but I cannot. I ask him to tell me to think otherwise, but he doesn't, and the distant voices of our enemies, whispered in bedrooms all over town, become the gathering threads of a current that pulls us east toward the mouth of the river.

NORTH

Rebecca Sawyer was the first person from Vaughn to score a perfect 1600 on the Scholastic Aptitude Test. When the news hit the *Valley Journal*, Mr. Sumner, her adviser, who had always said she was honors material and who had recommended on more than one occasion that she aim for state college, maybe for elementary education because she seemed to have the patience to work with children, marched her by the arm into his office. She had never been one of the best students in the class, not even in the top ten, but Mr. Sumner was also the boy's basketball coach, and Rebecca knew that in his world, where people were either starters or substitutes she had just been called off the bench. He spoke to her with half-time urgency. He flattened his hands on his desk and shook his head. He called her young lady. He was incredibly excited, he said, about her future.

Rebecca couldn't see how a score a few hundred points one way or another could have much of an affect on anyone's future, when five years before, a girl from Fort Kent, near the border of Quebec, had scored 1550, only to become a veterinarian's assistant.

"That's Fort Kent," Mr. Sumner said, pointing to his right, at a bookcase lined with trophies. "*This*," he said, pointing at his desk, "is Vaughn."

In the hall outside his office, a group of junior girls stopped talking as Rebecca walked by on her way to the bathroom where she stood alone in front of the mirror looking at herself. Next to the morning's article about her scores, the paper had printed a photo of her at her kitchen table. She had large dark eyes, dark hair, and a round face. Some people said she looked Italian or Portuguese; everyone agreed she looked nothing like her parents, grandparents, cousins, or aunts. The bell rang for the beginning of the next period but she kept staring. Some part of her was speaking to some other part of her, deciding something without her permission.

On her way into Mr. Cunningham's U.S. history class, she accidentally slammed the door and felt everyone look up as she crossed the room to her assigned seat by the window. Mr. Cunningham continued talking, referring to the reading from the night before while pointing to the board with yesterday's quizzes held curled in his fist. He asked what had happened in 1865, and looked from Rebecca to the left side of the room and back to her. Mention of the year brought the text before her mind as if onto a screen, the words scrolling down through her thoughts. She rarely spoke in class, but now, she felt, Mr. Cunningham and the other students waited for her to confess that she had always known the answers.

Rebecca's grandmother, Grandmame, was dying very slowly of old age, and every afternoon before dinner Rebecca spent a few minutes in her small room off the kitchen, which smelled of the hall closet and of burnt dust from the electric heater Grandmame turned all the way up. According to Rebecca's mother, it would have been cheaper for them to build their own power plant.

Rebecca sat in the green chair and looked with her Grandmame through the window across Central Street to the Methodist church and told her, as she did every day, how school went and what boys she liked. She made up the names of the boys.

"I thought of something to tell you," Grandmame said, "and now I can't remember. Well."

Grandmame removed her hand from Rebecca's and gripped the arm of her chair as if she were about to pull herself up.

"Have you heard anything from your brother?" Grandmame asked, and Rebecca shook her head. Grandmame asked this all the time, and the answer was always no. She dozed off again, her hands folded in her lap.

No one was allowed to speak of her brother in the house, except Grandmame, who did whatever she wanted. Even so, Grandmame always spoke about Jeremy in a whisper. Usually in the same breath she added that Rebecca's mother was cold. Everyone needed someone to blame, Rebecca supposed.

Jeremy's last visit, three months ago, had ended with a scene in the kitchen Rebecca would never forget. She didn't know how it started, or what the argument was about, but suddenly their mother's face turned red and she started screaming obscenities at the top of her voice. Jeremy's face drained for a moment, with his eyes closed, as if he had left his body, and then he flew through the air to punch their mother so hard in the face that her nose exploded with blood. Before Rebecca could even be sure what had happened, Jeremy ran out the door.

When he arrived home from work, her father cursed and threw his bag onto the kitchen table. "He can't keep running," he yelled from the living room where he stood looking out the window toward the river. He said he thought Jeremy had probably hopped the train and gone north, as he had the last time he ran away, to a tiny place called Dennis where he knew people. Her father said he didn't think there was much up there now, or since the end of the seventies when they stopped driving logs down the river. Maybe abandoned logger's camps and old farms. Probably squatters.

****

"I remember what I wanted to tell you," Grandmame said as Rebecca sat up. Rebecca thought it might be something new this time, even though Grandmame often got worked up over things she had just talked about the previous day. Rebecca was the only one who listened, and the only one Grandmame usually wanted to talk to.

"Not long after I was married to your grandfather, we bought this farm from a family who had seen trouble. I forget what kind now, money trouble. We gave them a good price I think, but they needed to sell in a hurry, so I believe we paid less than we might have."

Rebecca had heard this before and felt annoyed for a moment. The story went along as usual: the family they bought the house from had a daughter who died, and they came to Rebecca's grandparents asking to bury the girl in the graveyard. Their family had lived on the land for a hundred years. But Rebecca's grandfather said no.

Grandmame leaned over as if she believed this was the first time she was telling Rebecca. Each time she told it she reminded Rebecca not to tell anyone, not even her parents.

"One afternoon I was working in the garden when I found a patch of loose ground. I dug deeper with the trowel until I hit something hard. I thought it was a stone. That ground was full of stones when we bought the place. But when I cleared the dirt away, it was a girl's face. There was dirt in her mouth over her teeth, and over her eyelashes. Her skin was half rotted away. The smell was just the most horrible thing I had ever known. I went into the house for a sip of your grandfather's whiskey."

Grandmame paused, shaking her head. It seemed like she was catching her breath to continue. Rebecca tried to think of something to say to stop her from going on.

"I covered her up. I put my garden on top of her. What else could I do? If I told your grandfather, he would have dug her up. I'm the only one who knows she's there." Grandmame's face trembled slightly, and her eyes watered.

Rebecca rested her hand on Grandmame's arm. There was no girl buried in the ground. According to Rebecca's mother, the story had been circulating around the town for a hundred years, made up by the man who once owned the *Valley Journal* at the turn of the century as a Halloween tale for his daughter and her friends. It had been written up several years before to mark the anniversary of the paper.

Rebecca dressed and walked outside carrying her shoes. In the field behind the house, the morning light pinched her eyes and seemed to sap her strength. Wet grass slid between her toes; the sky at dawn had been orange, she could tell, from the white haze still on the horizon. The air held still for a moment over the farm, waiting for the late morning breeze to sweep up from the ocean into the valley. Maybe it would be warm, or the clouds might roll back from the coast. She stood there until the breeze came up, sending the maple and oak leaves into a boil. She was waiting, but for what she didn't know.

The school sat on top of the hill, its windows dark, as if no one were there, though she knew everyone was already in first period, lined up in rooms watching the teachers. Rebecca's friend Kathleen waited for her outside the front doors, in the usual place. Kathleen didn't care about being the smartest girl in school, she didn't even take the SAT, but Rebecca couldn't be sure how much would change between them now.

"I was about to give up on you," Kathleen said. "Smartest girl in school and she doesn't know what time it is." Kathleen shook her head disapprovingly. Rebecca started to apologize, but Kathleen raised her hand. "I always knew you were smart. Nothing you can do about it."

Rebecca was relieved that Kathleen thought being smart was a simple characteristic, like having hideous toes, that shouldn't change anything. And maybe in the past this had been true. Rebecca's father had told her that Grandmame was extremely smart, though you couldn't tell now. He described a time when he was young and his father was lecturing Grandmame on what was true and not true in state politics. She had embarrassed him after church by disagreeing with him in front of his friends. They were walking through the church parking lot, Grandmame yanking Rebecca's father along by the hand as her husband told her what was what. When they reached the end of the parking lot, Grandmame began reciting numbers at the top of her voice. At some point, Rebecca's father realized that Grandmame was listing the license plate numbers of all fifty cars in the church parking lot.

Rebecca's English teacher, Mrs. Lucas, called her up front after class and congratulated her, smiling thinly. Several other teachers did the same thing, but none of the students said anything at all. On the surface nothing changed, but people in the lunchroom seemed quieter when she passed, and when she sat down in the corner next to Kathleen, no one looked over at them. It wasn't what people would say, Rebecca realized, it was what they wouldn't say—even the teachers—as they tried to act naturally. Even Kathleen measured her words as she told a story about her boyfriend David's car breaking down. They were afraid now—of what, she couldn't be sure. Maybe of what she was thinking.

After school, while her mother was out shopping and her father was at work, Rebecca wandered through her parents' bedroom looking at the old pictures of her relatives, most of whom she had never met. She found a portrait of her grandfather standing outside the old barn in his overalls. Frozen in that single moment. She sat down on the edge of her parents' bed and looked at a picture of her brother Jeremy when he was five, leaning over the porch with his face covered in jam. In another picture, at their uncle's wedding, he stood at six years old in a blue blazer and yellow tie, already wearing their father's face. Five years older than her, he had always done things with her rather than make friends with boys his age. It was more of a problem when she started to make friends of her own, and didn't always want him around. She felt guilty about that now, and wanted to take each of those moments back.

She remembered once, she must have been six or a little older, when they were down at Boyton's Market, and Jeremy asked what she thought would happen if their parents both died. She was eating ice cream; it was summer. She didn't answer, had never thought of this before. Jeremy must have seen she looked worried because he told her not to worry. He had it figured out; they would be fine. He knew exactly what they would need and how they would get it.

"You promise?" she said.

He said of course he promised, and then she made him promise again because he had always said that one promise meant nothing but two meant you couldn't get out of it.

The first time her brother ran away was after a shouting match with their mother when he was sixteen. He came into Rebecca's bedroom the night he left and sat on the floor, running his hand down the length of his face. She was afraid to move as he rose on his knees as if he was going to pray.

"I don't know where I'll be," he whispered so lightly she wasn't even sure he wanted her to hear.

Even though he hadn't asked her to, she promised she would come find him, and then she promised him again.

A few hours before dawn, it started pouring outside her window. She had gone to bed early with an upset stomach, without eating dinner. She stood and pressed her forehead against the cold glass, looking into the backyard, and was not surprised that Jeremy wasn't leaning against the well house as the drops thudded against the hollow gutters. She had not wanted to admit for a long time that she knew things others could not know. It wasn't just about facts anyone could look up in a book. Now that the article had come out in the paper, everyone would suspect that she knew too much. When the photo of her grandfather in her parents' bedroom had been taken in 1955, for instance, she knew he was thinking of China Lake where he had grown up swimming with his two brothers. He was thinking of the lake because it was the tenth anniversary of his younger brother's death in the war. She knew this from looking into the photograph, into his dark eyes half-hidden behind his sagging lids. And she knew what her father would never admit, even to himself: that he no longer loved her mother; and she knew that her brother was going to die.

She didn't have the strength to move or say anything when her mother called up the stairs an hour
later and then came to sit on the edge of the bed, resting the back of her hand against Rebecca's cheek.

"You're burning up," her mother said. "I'll call."

Rebecca knew she wasn't sick—she just couldn't
stop thinking, which was a sickness no one could fix—
but she went along to the doctor's office where, in the
waiting room, her mother flipped through a *Good
Housekeeping*, snapping the pages so fast she could not
even have been looking at the pictures. Every time the
door to the nurse's area opened, her mother looked up,
startled, until finally she slammed the magazine shut
and swore. "Jesus." She looked at her watch and folded
her hands in her lap. Her mother often spoke to herself. She called it her therapy.

Rebecca stared wearily at her mother until her
mother looked up and shuddered.

"What?" her mother said. "What are you looking
at?" She stood up officiously and came over to sit next
to Rebecca and feel for her temperature again. "You're
still burning."

"I'm not sick," Rebecca said.

Rebecca followed the nurse to the examining room.
When the doctor arrived, his greeting was hollow,
echoing across the distance between his lips and his
attention. Rebecca had heard him saying goodbye to
the previous patient. She closed her eyes and opened

her mouth so he could examine her throat, and every muscle in her body seemed to relax.

"You had a fever last night and this morning," he said. She nodded. His breath brushed her neck as he leaned over to look inside her mouth. He asked her to tilt her neck slightly and she did. He rested a hand next to her leg on the table and pressed his fingers against her neck below her jaw.

He told her she might have a small infection but didn't think she needed antibiotics, at least not yet. In the car her skin seemed to vibrate where the doctor had touched her, like a trivial memory that would not go away, and when her mother asked, Rebecca told her what the doctor had said. For that, her mother replied, we pay him.

Rebecca's father had once said of her mother when no one else was around that she would never let them forget she was from Portland.

Rebecca told herself there was no point in going—she could not change what would happen—yet she had to. She waited until early morning. Her father had said Jeremy jumped the train and rode it all the way up until he reached Dennis, so that's what she would do.

In the hours before dawn, the train moved slowly in the heavy air, the lights from Water Street flashing between boxcars. As she had seen boys from school do, she ran along a granite wall that paralleled the tracks and jumped up on the floor of one of the cars, landing in the cool inside where the clicking of the metal wheels amplified in the empty drum. The train followed the river for ten or twelve miles before crossing over in Gardner and heading north out of the valley into the rich smell of the tidal banks. She leaned against the frame and looked at the black trees in the blue glow of the woods. Only now did she find the tear in the knee of her pants and in the skin underneath, which seemed the only evidence that she had made it this far.

The half-moon passed in and out of the clouds, giving brief glimpses of her white sneakers. The train slowed before each town and sped up as it snaked back into the woods where for several minutes she couldn't see the tops of her hands. The air in her chest seemed to vibrate with the floor of the boxcar, turning each breath into a gasp. She would not be able to scream if she had to, and even if she could, no one would hear her above the scraping of the wheels over the tracks. Jeremy must have felt, as she did now, that he was in the grip of an iron fist that would not let go.

She fell asleep curled up and woke to see the train stretching through a bend in the mist. The sun just struggling through lit up the rust-red boxcars. At one crossing a man standing with a paper bag took off his hat and laughed when he saw her. She hung out of the door by her arm and looked up the track where tree branches arched over the train. Finally, she saw a green sign for DENNIS. The train wasn't moving very fast, but it was frightening to jump and roll in the grass when she didn't know what lay underneath. She rose to her feet and ran for a dirt road, where she turned just in time to see the caboose rocking on its narrow perch.

A half-mile down she thought she saw a gas station and a store on the other side of the road, but there were no people or cars, nothing to suggest a town. Maybe this was the edge of town and she had jumped too soon. She walked in the direction of the gas station, scuffing her sneakers through the dirt. Part of her hoped she did have the wrong place, because if she found him she would have to say something. She never wanted to be the one to speak and hated the feeling of people looking at her, waiting for what she would say, for her thoughts, for what she knew. People were greedy. They pretended not to want things, they pretended not to care, except for Jeremy, who never pretended he didn't need anything from anyone. He needed her to look for him.

A truck approached from behind, sending up a plume of dust as the driver steered with his right hand on top of the wheel, his chin pulled in. Messy clumps of hair stuck out beneath his cap. She expected the truck to drive on to the store, but instead it took a left and crawled over a driveway toward a low farmhouse once painted white and since worn to a rotting gray. She knew Jeremy was inside. It had been this simple for him: jumping off the train, finding an abandoned house. This was the way he did everything, choosing what was in front of him as if there was no other choice.

She stopped walking several times in order to think more clearly, and once almost turned around, though she sensed with resignation that turning around would lead to the same place, in the end, as going through the open front door of the house. A box of rusty tools sat in the front hall and the air felt breathed and rebreathed by the cracked and buckling plaster. A gas can leaned against the wall. In the living room one of two windows was open to the field behind the house where the tall grass bent under a breeze and pushed up again. It seemed impossible that the world outside, where the air moved through the light, was at all connected to the world inside this house, and it wasn't right that she had been able to pass so easily between the two. Jeremy lay on a battered couch with his arms at his sides, his eyes closed. She thought he must be sleeping, but then his eyes snapped open and stared at her as if he didn't know her and she had come to take everything away from him. Small bottles, a plate, and a leather belt sat on an upturned box at his feet. She said his name, but he did not say her name back or change his expression in any way. When he swallowed, a cleft appeared in his chin and the veins of his neck pushed against his translucent skin. His Adam's apple fluttered as his eyes closed, and his chest rose and fell to the timing of heels clomping down the stairs behind her. When no one appeared, she thought the pounding had come from her own head, but the man she had just seen in the truck stepped from around the corner with his hands in his jeans pockets, the leather cap on his head. He quickly removed his glasses to clean them on his T-shirt. He said he was hoping she would come by.

"How do you know who I am?"

"How did you know which house to walk into?" He put the glasses back on and looked at her. He was probably her brother's age or a bit older. He sat in the chair next to the couch, crossed his legs, and put on the face of someone trying to look like a college student, with his chin resting on his hand. His sharp lips chopped off the consonants when he spoke, sounding to her like one of the migrant worker's kids.

"I'm not from around here like my friend," he said, as if this should explain any questions she might have. He leaned back and clasped his hands behind his head with his elbows in the air.

"You're not his friend!" Rebecca shouted in what could not have been her voice.

"Whatever you say." He shrugged one shoulder and glanced over at Jeremy who seemed to see through them. "We've got everything you need here to be happy. We've got food if that's what you need, we've got money, we've got a roof that don't leak—and we've got *business* coming right down from Canada. This here's a stop on the Trans-Canada highway." He looked at her brother for a moment before turning to her and reaching in his jacket pocket to pull out a photo in which she thought she could see her brother and herself when they were younger, but she quickly looked away and shook her head. She couldn't breathe.

"That's my favorite picture," he said, saying it *pisure*, while looking away, as if embarrassed. He sighed and dropped his shoulders into the silence that followed and lasted until he seemed smaller than her. "That's at Niagara Falls. I've never been there, but I want to go, I plan to go. In fact, I could go right now if I wanted to. There's nothing stopping me."

"I have to go," she said and then watched him, waiting to see if he would try to stop her.

"Suit yourself." He closed his eyes and slid further down in the chair.

Jeremy turned to face the wall, and she opened her mouth to call out to him—if she just said his name, maybe he would come back with her, though of course he wouldn't. If she said his name, he might explode, as he had that morning at her mother. He didn't want to attack her—the idea would never occur to him—but whatever pushed from the inside against his rising and falling back hated everything, even her.

Outside, she ran across the overgrown field for the road and the tracks, stopping only to catch her breath and look over her shoulder. No one followed. The tracks were empty, running between the fields and into the woods both in the direction from which she had come and where the train was still headed, all the way north, she assumed, to Canada. Everywhere she looked, down either direction of the tracks or across the field into the woods, she saw the starved image of Jeremy's face. She ran for a few more minutes, stopping when she could no longer breathe, to bend over her knees and make a sound in her throat like the wheels of her father's car crunching over the gravel of their driveway.

A train would come eventually, if she kept walking in the direction of home, and if she kept her thoughts straight and parallel to the glinting edge of the rail, which drew her under a canopy of turning leaves. The tips of her sneakers slid forward over the chattering gravel until she was convinced the noise came from Jeremy or the other one following her, and she started to run again until she reached a bridge where the woods opened above a river.

She thought she saw something moving through the trees to the right but instead of going back or freezing (as she told herself to do), she ran toward it, jumping over fallen trees and yelling Jeremy's name. She stopped in a clearing above a stream and looked around, but there was nothing there. The blue sky paled around the edges. Pockets of warmth drifted in the cool air. She looked down the slope, feeling as though she could see inside the wind brushing through the grass. The distant pines leaned together in a sudden gust and were still again. When the breeze returned, it seemed to whistle through her limbs, and she realized that Jeremy had been here, in this clearing, in the grass. He had measured the wind by the movement of the branches.

The train whistle bleated as it passed through Dennis, and she bolted toward the sound. The wheels ground against the rails, ticking off what little time she had left to get home before they knew where she had gone and what she had seen. The boxcars moved through the trees, speeding up as if the forest was rushing south. Some of the Boston-Maine cars were empty, doors slid back on both sides, the sunlight blinking through the openings as she ran to the bridge along a platform from where she leapt half onto the edge of a car. Inside, with her face pressed to the cold metal, she sensed him: Jeremy's face with the stranger's hat and long arms, both of them in the same body standing in one of the dark corners. She looked for their smile, and their eyes, glowing in the shadow, but there was nothing.

The train slowed into each town, the tracks occasionally winding within fifteen feet of backyards and kitchen windows. It was not hard for her to determine the characters and even the thoughts of the people living inside the houses. People wanted you to think things were complicated when they weren't. The train passed close to the window of someone's kitchen where a woman looked up from doing the dishes. She's thinking about her twelve-year-old son, Rebecca thought, who was caught stealing from a corner store. All the information was around her in the air, waiting for her to absorb it. Her own mother was frightened and vain;

she always had been and she always would be. Her father was patient and simple near the surface and unhappy underneath. It couldn't be any different than the facts she learned for tests: Pablo Picasso, born October 25, 1881. His first painting *La fillette aux pieds nus*. 1895. A poem she glanced at two weeks before, the "Song of Apollo," with the second stanza, "Then I arise; and climbing Heaven's blue dome, I walk over the mountains and the wave . . . I am the eye with which the Universe Beholds itself, and knows it is divine." The earth was formed 4.6 billion years ago. The words cesium, curium, erbium, rhodium, argon, osmium, streamed through her head faster than the trees whipping by outside.

She remembered a story her mother told of being a girl in the nineteen fifties and traveling on a freighter across the Atlantic to Europe with her father, who was a merchant marine. There was a storm—a hurricane— her mother had said, and described the ship rising up the mountainous waves, the wind faster than if you put your hand out of the car window on the highway. Her mother had been much younger than Rebecca was now, and as her mother's father helped on the deck of the freighter, she sat alone in the dark cabin. Rebecca had heard her mother tell this story dozens of times over the years, and each time her mother stuck out her chin and wore a blank, put-upon face. Each time, Rebecca mistook her mother's expression for boredom, as if she was being forced to tell the story again even though no one had asked her to. Now Rebecca could see the expression was thinly disguised pride. Rebecca's father realized this, too, which was why he complained every time that it wasn't actually a hurricane. "All right, it *wasn't*," her mother shouted at him one night in front of people from his work who were having dinner at their house. She stood up from the table with tears in her eyes. "It wasn't, okay, it wasn't *officially* a hurricane if that makes you happy. I was ten years old down in a square metal room with no lights or windows and with the boat practically upside down, back and forth for eighteen hours!" Her mother turned and left the table but came back in a moment to apologize and laugh lightly. "My, my," she said when she sat, refolding her napkin. "You'll have to excuse me."

Her mother had been terrified in that room, holding onto the edge of a metal bunk as everything lurched back and forth and the inner workings of the boat groaned. When Rebecca closed her eyes, she could see her mother clinging in the dark compartment with no idea if they would survive or if she would see her father again. The noises of the ship would not have been much different than the noises of the boxcars knocking together as she sped through the woods.

The crossing bells went off one after another as she drew closer to Vaughn, and she expected someone she knew, a friend of her mother or her guidance counselor, to look up from their gardening or their steering wheel to see her face in the open door of the boxcar. When she leapt from the train onto the grass near the town library, she expected the bell at the Catholic church up the street to ring for the six p.m. service or the Baptist church for their seven p.m. service or at least the more distant sound of the town hall clock bell sounding on the hour. But it wasn't Sunday night, there were no services, and it wasn't on the hour. She sat on the grass watching the train pick up speed as it left town, the lights of the caboose fading into the darkening pines, and the crossing bells growing silent, one after another, in the distance.

In the kitchen, the heat from her mother's cooking clung to her cheeks and palms.

"I put all the dish towels in the laundry. Would you grab me one from upstairs?"

Rebecca nodded.

"You're home late," her mother called after her.

"I was at Kathleen's."

"Hurry up and wash your hands and you can help me set the table."

Her mother took the forks and spoons, moving back and forth deftly between the stove and the table with the same urgency she brought to every night's dinner.

"Okay," her mother said after everyone sat, reaching out to take Rebecca's and Grandmame's hands. "Someone say grace, please."

As Rebecca's father started, her mother squeezed Rebecca's hand so hard the bones of her fingers pinched together. Her mother pulled her jaw in and cinched her eyes shut, tears welling up over her bottom lids and washing down her face. She always feels so much, it's as if she feels for all of us, Rebecca thought.

"I think I'm coming down with the flu," her mother said. "I'll go lie down for a while." She plucked her hands away from them and stood up from the table as if from an insult.

"Do you want one of us to come with you, with some food?" her father said. "There is something going around at work. Maybe you have it."

Rebecca knew from the tone of his voice that he didn't think she had the flu, and that he had no intention of comforting her.

"Go ahead and eat," her mother said.

Grandmame stared across the room for a few minutes while her father unfolded his napkin and arranged his silverware in a perfect row.

"Don't let your mother's hard work go to waste," he said as he started cutting into the pork chop. After a few more minutes, after Grandmame had started eating, humming faintly to herself, as she sometimes did, a tune no one recognized and which probably wasn't a real tune at all, her father leaned back and asked Rebecca what she had done at school that day.

"Nothing," she said.

"Nothing?" he said, raising his eyebrows. "Well, that's good. They're getting you used to the working world. You've got three and a half hours—less a coffee break or two—of nothing before lunch, but you don't want to use it all up before lunch because you've got a good four of nothing after lunch. And then you want to be careful to have people see you shove nothing in your briefcase at the end of the day so they think you're doing nothing at home, too." He smiled through this, amused with himself.

Grandmame went back to her room while Rebecca helped her father carry the dishes to the sink. He scraped the plates that she handed to him and stacked them neatly in one side of the double sink with the silverware piled in a basket. She was just turning back to the table for the salad bowl when he started humming a song she didn't recognize. He caught her arm and pulled her toward him, swaying from left to right in a dance he must have learned before she was born—she had never seen him dance. A smile spread up from his chin until his whole face lifted, and he opened his eyes and chuckled before letting go, turning off the water, and picking up the *Valley Journal* from the counter on his way to the living room.

"What about the rest of the dishes?" she asked.

"Leave them, I'll do them later," he said, raising the back of his hand, though she knew he wouldn't. "Go check on your mother."

Her mother lay on top of the covers in the dark bedroom, her arms spread wide, and her eyes closed. Rebecca thought she was asleep.

"Come here," her mother said, holding her hands out like a child wanting to be picked up. Rebecca pulled back at first but then held her hands out. Her mother's crying passed up into her own arms and across the back of her neck.

"He's not coming back, is he?" her mother said. "It's going to be winter soon. It will be so cold up there."

"Of course he's coming back," Rebecca lied, tumbling forward from the weight. Her mother wrapped an arm around her shoulder and squeezed as she buried her face in Rebecca's neck. The smell of her mother's hair was both familiar and distant, like the sight of her brother's face, and the harder her mother squeezed, the more Rebecca felt as if she were far away from this moment, floating over their house and town.

"Please, promise me you won't ever become mixed up with the people your brother did."

"I won't," she said.

"Of course you won't," her mother said. "You're too smart for that."

Her mother rolled onto her back, lifted her hand to her forehead, and sighed. Rebecca waited for what she would say—when her mother lost control, she talked frantically afterward to cover it up.

"I don't know why I was thinking about your brother tonight," her mother said. "Before dinner I was remembering a sailing trip your father and I took right before we were married, when I was already pregnant with your brother. Grandmame didn't even want us to get married, I don't suppose there's any harm in telling you now—because I wasn't Catholic—and she did not approve of taking a trip like that before the wedding, but the wedding was in the fall—it had to be, I forget why, I guess because I was already pregnant. I don't know how we thought we were going to fool that woman. The trip was up the coast on an old tall ship. We sailed for ten days with three other couples. Every evening before dusk the captain and the crew anchored in a small harbor, and while they put everything away and made us supper, we sat on the deck and looked out at the ocean. We had absolutely nothing to do. I knew it would be rare in the life we were starting, but your father, who had worked on the farm from the day he started walking until he started college, couldn't understand why anyone would want to sit still for so long staring at the sky and the water. I think the whole thing was torture for him. One evening before dinner, he stood up beside me, stripped down to his boxers, and dove off the bow. It was as if he just couldn't sit still any longer and he had to make some work for himself. Watching the bottoms of his feet disappear, I just lost it for a moment. It was stupid, but I thought he wouldn't come back up—that he was running away from me. That time on the boat was the longest we had ever spent together, and I felt this desperation of not wanting to lose him. When I saw him crash up a little ways out, shivering and waving with a big smile on his face, I was so happy, I almost jumped in after him, and I probably would have if that water wasn't cold enough to stop your breath forever."

Her mother fell silent with her arms at her sides. Her toes and fingers twitched after a few minutes as her breath settled into the rhythm of sleep. Rebecca listened for her father's footsteps, but she could tell from the distant flutter of a turning page that he was still down in the living room reading the paper.

Rebecca stared at the bedroom ceiling and imagined standing with her mother as her father swam back to the boat and climbed up the ladder. Her father dressed, hopping on one leg, and whispered something in her mother's ear as she bent over, laughing. Rebecca had never seen her mother laugh this way before. Her parents put their arms around each other and walked toward the stern as if Rebecca wasn't there because, of course, she wasn't. Then her father ran back toward Rebecca, but only for his jacket, which lay at her feet, and when he glanced up, there was no look of recognition on his face. Rebecca knew this feeling, had known it all along, of not being seen, but she would also remember the look on her father's face that told of how even this brief moment away from his new wife was too much to bear.

Rebecca went to bed, falling immediately asleep without undressing, and didn't know what time it was when she sat straight up and looked out the dark window. Her clock radio was unplugged, probably from when her mother vacuumed, and her limbs felt heavy as she padded down into the kitchen. The moon hung low in the sky, everything silent except the dormant sounds of the house, the refrigerator, and the furnace in the basement.

"Rebecca, is that you?" Grandmame called from her room. Even though Grandmame rose before dawn, she kept the blinds tightly drawn at night and the room pitch black, so that Rebecca had trouble finding her way to the ratty green chair.

"Is that you?" Grandmame said again. She was only a foot away in her narrow bed, but Rebecca couldn't see her face.

"It's me," she said.

"There was something I wanted to tell you after dinner, but I didn't get the chance."

Instead of going on, though, Grandmame's breathing calmed, and the airless room filled with the musk of her skin and clothes. Rebecca leaned her head back and pictured herself on the train headed north toward Jeremy. She tried to remember his face in that house but could only see the strain of his neck and the cleft where there had not been one before. The harder she tried to remember his face, the more he looked like someone she didn't know. She thought of what her mother had said about winter coming. In one afternoon of snow, everything she had seen up there—the pines, the field, and the low house—would be sheeted white against a white sky. He wouldn't stay in Dennis for long, she guessed, and he wouldn't come back to Vaughn. He would continue north on the train, hundreds of miles through the thick forest until there was nothing but rock covered with ice. She pictured him there, as far up as anyone could go, walking across a blank white plain extending out to the horizon. Her brother, she realized, had gone north not to run away from life, as her father had said, but to know everything. Because he had wanted her to follow, she would have to keep looking for him, even if she would never find him, and even if he was no longer there but somehow everywhere, all around them.

Grandmame shook Rebecca's leg, and Rebecca opened her eyes to the morning light framing the shade.

"An awful, awful thing has happened," Grandmame said in such an urgent voice that Rebecca leaned forward to hear. But then Rebecca realized her Grandmame was about to tell the tale, once again, that she had read in the newspaper of the girl who had been buried in a backyard. There was nothing Rebecca could say to stop her, so she just listened and waited for the story to end.

"I was only six years old when they buried me," Grandmame said as tears soaked the moth wings of her cheeks. "My father wanted to put me next to his mother, but the people who bought the farm from us wouldn't let him, so he dug my grave in their vegetable garden while they were sleeping, and no one knows. No one knows where I am."

The train whistle blew in the distance, the first warning of its approach from the north. Rebecca felt the air shiver from the force of the locomotive against the tracks as the second whistle blew and echoed down the valley, carried on its way south by the tide. The third whistle blew the final warning, though to Rebecca it was less a warning than a cry.

"I don't want to be buried in this place," Grandmame said and squeezed hard on Rebecca's arm. "Promise me you won't let them."

A promise was easy to give, and as Rebecca whispered it, Grandmame sighed as if she had finally been relieved of an unbearable secret.

AFTERNOON OF THE *SASSANOA*

Jacob's father had business in town that afternoon and the next morning. "Go with him," Jacob's mother said. "You two can spend the night and sign up for your pre-season soccer in the morning before coming back. It will save me having to give you a ride down."

Jacob agreed to go, even though it took him away from the island and involved a trip with his father across to the mainland in the skiff and a seemingly endless hour's drive. Not bothering to bring a change of clothes, Jacob jumped off the back porch and followed his father down to the island's dock.

The fetch between Heron Island and the mainland darkened as Jacob's father, in the stern, thumbed tobacco into his pipe. After a few attempts he gave up trying to light the pipe in the wind, and as if this failure tumbled him toward another, he pushed away from the dock and started to row from the wrong direction, pushing the handles away from his chest. Jacob was in the oarsman's seat, and it was harder for his father, rowing this way, to keep the leathers from popping out of the locks. The bags under his father's eyes looked even heavier than usual, and a thin line of blood traced across his freshly shaved neck. His shoulders bunched as he reached forward, his already round face growing red and puffy after only a few strokes.

"You take it." His father pushed the oar handles toward Jacob. Even though it was not far to the dock on the mainland, they would blow downwind, toward Robinhood Cove, unless Jacob pulled as hard as he could. As a way of not looking at his father's face, he gazed through the Townsend Gut, the narrowest point between the island and the main, where the water funneled in and the wind whipped between the columns of tall pines, kicking up rows of chop.

"It's the best day for sailing we've had yet," his father said. Jacob shot a glance at the *Sassanoa* riding high on her white hull above the water, her nose pointing into the wind and jumping up like a thoroughbred against her mooring tether.

"Let's go for a short sail, just once across the bay, and then I'll still have time to get to town."

"I thought you had to be there by four. We might not even make it if we start now."

"By five, five thirty. I just have to meet the guy to have him sign some papers and have someone take them over to the courthouse in Augusta before it closes."

Jacob didn't say anything. He had already said enough to his mother about not wanting to go to town. He wanted to sign up for soccer, but he hated anything that took him away from the island. Also, he and his father would be alone for the night, and then Jacob would have to hang around the house all day, waiting for his father to finish work so they could make the trip back to the island.

He wondered if it was a good idea for his father not to leave enough time to get his client to sign the papers, and he knew when his father rushed he always drove too fast, and sometimes got a ticket. That would put him in a foul mood for the whole week. Jacob didn't want to say anything about not sailing, didn't want to screw up his chances of taking the boat out alone the next year, while his father was at work, when he could sail by himself down the coast to Five Islands. The tourists there, eating lobsters and clams, would look at him as though he had stepped into their lives from a past century. The year before, his father had said he could take the boat out when he was twelve, the same age at which Jacob's grandfather had let his father go out alone, but this year his father changed his mind to thirteen. Jacob wasn't sure he would ever be old enough at this rate.

"We'll just go across the bay and back," his father said and nodded in the direction of the *Sassanoa*. Jacob pushed harder on the port oar and swung them around.

The day was good for sailing. The pines swayed; the breeze was southerly but cool. Jacob started to row for the island dock. His father's hand shot forward and wrapped around the starboard oar, shoving it into Jacob's chest so hard that it knocked the wind out of him.

"What about the life jackets in the boat bag?" Jacob asked.

"We're just going across the bay once."

His father looked away, apparently realizing he had accidentally been too rough. Jacob wasn't going to argue about the boat bag. Even his grandfather had gone without it on short sails—just to spite the yacht-club guys and their overprecautions, he would say. Jacob's father opened his briefcase for the mobile phone (as large, with the battery, as a cracker box) and pushed POWER, bringing the clear buttons to life with yellow light. He dialed and held the phone to his head while reaching out with the other hand to grab the *Sassanoa*. Frustrated, he handed the phone to Jacob.

"When your mother picks up tell her we're just going across the bay and back before we head to Vaughn."

Jacob took the phone. His father rested his briefcase on the deck of the *Sassanoa*, balanced himself precariously on the seat of the skiff, and pulled himself up. Both Jacob and his mother hated having a phone on the island, where they came to escape these things, and his mother was already upset about his father rushing to Vaughn three days into his late August vacation, for an emergency meeting.

"You don't have your windbreaker," his mother said, after Jacob told her what they were doing.

"It's warm out."

"Tell her we're not going to be out long."

Jacob's mother heard her husband. "So call me from town tonight," she said. Jacob didn't know what to say. He said goodbye, his mother said goodbye, and he replaced the receiver in the battery case.

Jacob couldn't remember a time when they had not come to the island in the summer. Jacob often helped his mother scrub the clothes against the washboard in the back of the cottage, using water they caught from the sky and stored in a large tank. Jacob's grandfather had been the pilot of Portland Harbor and both his grandparents had lived on the island year-round without insulation or anything else the cabin still didn't have—things that Jacob wished their house in Vaughn didn't have either. Sometimes in the fall, after returning to Vaughn, Jacob refused to use the phone, lights, or running water, as a way of pretending he was still on the island.

As if they were trying to escape, or as if the rush that Jacob expected on the road had already begun, his father tugged frantically at the sail ties, pulling out the boom crutch and tossing it carelessly under the foredeck, whereas Jacob had been taught to lash it forward to keep it from banging around while under way.

Things were done in a certain manner on the island, not only because they had been done that way for sixty years but because it was the right way. Jacob had learned everything about the island from his grandfather. Now that his grandfather was gone, Jacob sometimes wondered if his father was forgetting things. The previous fall Jacob had had to remind him to spread wood chips beneath the *Sassanoa* in the boathouse, to absorb moisture through the winter. The old oak planks, cut from trees on the island, would get dry rot in one season without the wood chips, and he worried that his father did not think of it.

"Just tie the skiff up now," his father yelled. They had always tied the skiff to the stern until the *Sassanoa* was ready to sail. Otherwise the two boats would rub. Jacob moored the skiff to the buoy, as he had been told, and of course his father had not raised the main by then, so he had to sit on the deck and separate the two boats with his legs. His father tugged on the halyard, but it was stuck.

"Damn," his father grumbled. "Jacob, help me for a second." Jacob was reluctant to let the two boats rub, but his father was frustrated, so Jacob pushed the skiff off as far from the sailboat's hull as he could and rushed back to hold the halyard while his father jiggled the runner free. The sail rose easily then, snapping at the air, and Jacob rushed back to the bow to find the rail of the skiff already rubbing against the *Sassanoa*'s white hull. He swore to himself, pushed the dory away, and leaned over the bow to see what damage had been done. He saw a scratch three inches long. It hadn't penetrated to the wood, but the skiff had gouged out several layers of paint and left a green smudge. It would allow moisture closer to the wood. He should fix the scratch right away, as his grandfather had taught him to do, though the only way to really take a scratch out was to haul the *Sassanoa* and repaint the entire hull. Jacob was trying not to think about it, but he knew they shouldn't sail now. Not with a scratch in the hull.

"Cast off," his father yelled. The sail was up, but the tiller was still lashed. Jacob untied the bowline but did not let go of the mooring buoy until his father freed the tiller. Then they drifted back with the wind until the sail scooped the air and leaned them to port. It was a perfect breeze. With the jib up they would move along nicely. The *Sassanoa* never moved very fast. She was nineteen feet on the waterline and modeled after a Friendship Sloop, with full keel and wide beam; Jacob's great grandfather had designed her to transport his family and their supplies to and from shore.

Jacob raised the jib and tied down the sheet; his father held the tiller and the main sheet, so there was nothing for Jacob to do except watch the skiff at the mooring become smaller as they tacked back and forth in the narrow space between the island and the mainland. As they came through the Gut around the end of the island and faced the bay, the sails braced against the wind coming off the ocean. His father loosened the main, leaned back, and eyed the telltales. The telltales had been his father's addition, after his grandfather's death, and Jacob knew they weren't right. He never looked at them when he sailed, but felt the boat's movement under him to find the wind. If the breeze was stiff but he felt no tension on the tiller and little heel, he was off the wind. His grandfather had taught him to rely as little as possible on sight. Eyes were no good in fog or darkness.

"I bet we can make the lighthouse in one tack," his father said. Jacob tried to gauge how the wind and tide would take them over the three quarters of a nautical mile. The wind was shifting around to the southwest, so they could head farther out, but then Jacob wondered how long it would take for them to get back. If the wind stayed southerly, or even if it moved completely westerly, they would have no problem on a broad reach plowing straight across the bay. Jacob looked around for the coast guard, but the bay was empty except for a few lobster boats and a trawler. They often sailed across the bay without the boat bag—the *Sassanoa* could handle any kind of rough weather that might come up unexpectedly. But the coast guard had fined them twice for not having life jackets; his father had tried to argue out of the ticket each time.

Jacob looked back at the granite face of Heron Island, jutting south like the prow of a ship. His mother was working beside the house on the island, taking the laundry in off the line. Inside the cabin his dead grandfather stared down with cold eyes at the dining-room table from the framed photo on the wall. Jacob assumed it was the circumstances of the time that had made him hard. Jacob remembered when he had rowed over to the island with his grandfather in the winter to cut down a Christmas tree; the steam had risen from the water in white patches like ghosts and blown with the wind across the bay. The scene had seemed medieval; the cracked brown knuckles of his grandfather's hands moved toward him and away, rowing. Jacob had removed his glove and dipped his hand in the water, which felt warm, like a bath, compared with the air.

Even now, Jacob thought, the year could have been 1878 on the island—nothing about the kerosene lamps or cast-iron pots suggested that people elsewhere had ever seen electricity, and in the weeks they spent on the island each summer, Jacob forgot about the appliances of their house in Vaughn, where his father rose and dressed in a suit each morning before driving off to his small office on Water Street.

"Haul in the jib," his father snapped, and Jacob obeyed even though he knew the jib would not come in any farther without spilling air and losing some of what his father wanted, which was to point higher so they could reach the lighthouse in one tack. His father pulled in the main sheet, running the line down around the cleat. The *Sassanoa* heeled over in response. Rollers from a storm that had never reached shore pitched them up. Jacob did not worry. He and his grandfather had been out in fifty-knot winds. The ribs and planks creaked but nothing gave, not even the old hand-sewn sails. But the boat was weaker now, since his grandfather's death.

As they approached the lighthouse, Jacob saw tourists standing on the rocks raise their binoculars to examine them. The *Sassanoa* was an unusual sight, with its mahogany bright work on deck, its white hull and blood-red sails, the spars themselves varnished spruce, cut from the forest on the mainland less than a mile from the island. Jacob saw a boy about his age borrow binoculars from his father and look out, and Jacob envied the boy for looking at the boat, though he would rather be where he was, sailing her. She sailed very nicely, not fast like these new fiberglass boats built with long fin keels and flat bottoms. Those were good for speed, but not for rollers and sudden winds. Jacob would take the *Sassanoa* in any bad weather over one of those ugly boats. The *Sassanoa* rolled over the swells and did not slap the spray back into the cockpit. A powerful, curling swell could punch a hole in the side of a glass hull, but the *Sassanoa*'s thick oak planks absorbed each blow like a prizefighter feeling for his opponent's strength.

"Let's sail over to Mauldin," his father said. "From there it'll be a straight shot back in."

Jacob looked down at his watch. "I don't know if you'll have time to make it into town if we don't head back now."

"It won't make much difference," his father called, looking up at the sail. "We can't miss a wind like this."

"I don't think we'll have enough time," Jacob said again, staring at the floorboards.

Instead of getting angry, as Jacob expected, his father smiled as he looked up at the sail. "A wind like this will take us anywhere." Jacob looked at his father and saw his crooked yellow teeth and bumpy nose, the swell of fat girdling his jaw. For the first time, he saw his father as he imagined a woman might see him, in the clear, unforgiving sunlight.

Jacob glanced up toward the southwestern sky at a line of thick dark clouds moving toward them with the freshening wind. Already his father had to ease off on the main sheet to accommodate the extra force. Thunderheads. "Head for shore when you see those," his grandfather had said.

After a long track they came up on the high granite side of Mauldin Island. Some people in a house above sat on their porch looking in the direction of the thunderheads, probably discussing if they should secure the shutters. It was hard to predict what the weather would do, even when they could see it coming, but finally Jacob mentioned it.

"What about those thunderheads?"

"Those are thunderheads," his father said matter-of-factly. No smile this time. Suddenly, as a small cloud shaded the sun, his father looked down into the green water at the small ripples curling into the windward side of the hull. He seemed to be concentrating on a difficult decision.

The bow of the *Sassanoa* ploughed through the water toward the rocks. The shallows dropped off immediately, but they were closing fast, fifteen yards, twelve, and his father still looked over the windward side. Jacob determined not to say anything and almost found himself hoping the boat would crash into the granite. He shook his head at the thought. Five yards away his father casually swung the tiller across and brought them about. Jacob unhitched the jib and cleated it on the starboard side. He readied himself to let the sail out for heading downwind, but his father kept them headed out of the bay, straight for New Wagon harbor.

"I thought we were going to head in," Jacob said, trying not to sound anxious.

"I thought we would head out and sail through the 'trickiest bit of sailing in the East,'" his father said, quoting Jacob's grandfather. His father gave a quick nod in the direction they were heading, and Jacob saw the corner of his mouth rise as he leaned down to pull in the mainsheet.

"What about your client and signing those papers?"

"Fuck it. Just fuck it."

Jacob waited for him to say more, but his father studied the luff in the canvas where the main joined the mast. "Winds like this don't come around every day." He narrowed his eyes, pulling in on the sheet and carefully adjusting the tiller. Jacob had never seen him look so determined, not even when he worked. "We can make New Wagon harbor in one tack."

Jacob wondered about his father's work, if people would be left waiting in town and if they would be angry at his father. Jacob had heard conversations over the last months between his mother and father about his father's practice, and Jacob was not sure everything was going well.

New Wagon harbor, on the southern tip of a peninsula, was formed by three small, burly islands nestled close into shore. They sailed within ten yards of the mainland on the port side, trying to edge into the harbor without tacking again. Jacob could see the pale, sharp rocks below the tidal line, and the red keel that edged up toward the surface as they heeled over.

"How much room we got?" his father asked.

"You got it," Jacob answered.

"One tack."

They were inside the harbor, the mainland and dock to the left, the three islands to the right, and Jacob felt relieved. As if a hand had released its pressure on the mast, they tilted upright as the wind diminished behind the islands.

That wasn't the trickiest bit of sailing, though. Now they were going to sail between the northern and eastern islands, where unmarked rocks spiked up from the bottom. Jacob thought the tide was too low, which was the only thing that had made his grandfather describe this ledge as tricky. They simply needed to know where the rocks were and to go at the right tide.

"Our momentum will carry us until we can catch the wind again," his father said. "And I'll steer us around the rocks."

Jacob nodded, though he was doubtful. They couldn't see the rocks beneath the surface, but his father had sailed this many times before, with his father and alone. Jacob didn't know how shallow it would be. The rollers crashed into the windward side of the islands, but the water in the harbor was calm.

"Pull the jib in," his father said. Wind would come around the island and they would heel, so they would draw less. That would help.

On his father's orders, Jacob uncleated the jib, tightened it, and recleated it, but there was no point—the jib had been lashed too tight to begin with.

"Good." His father pulled in on the mainsheet, preparing for the wind. The tide was moving out, lowering every minute now. Several families were eating lunch on the pier outside the Lobster Shack. They stopped cracking their lobsters for a moment to stare at the red sails of the *Sassanoa* gliding by from sheer momentum on the flat water. One of the youngest children leapt up when she saw the sails and raced toward the end of the pier. Her mother ran after, yelling the girl's name. The girl could have run off the end of the pier. She stopped at the last minute, though, and pointed at the red sails.

Jacob could see twelve, ten yards ahead, the line of blue water marking the wind. As they grew closer, the wind receded and the shallow rocks appeared, yellow and white beneath the surface. Jacob watched the blue patch of wind on the water draw back like a snake into its hole and vanish. Now they were drifting straight toward the rocks with no wind coming around the island to make them heel. His father knew and only had a few seconds to decide what they would do. He could gradually steer them to port, but without wind there was no point in throwing the tiller over. They would still drift forward. Before either could act or speak Jacob saw just behind his father's head a patch of dark blue water, a stiff gust, advancing from the north. Jacob barely had time to release the jib, though he realized later that it was the wrong thing to do. The wind caught inside the loose jib and lurched them straight forward at no heel. His father lowered his jaw and put his hands out to the side as if some enormous creature had lifted him off the ground and was preparing to swallow him whole. Jacob waited for the sound, but halfway through the passage none had come, and he thought maybe they would make it all the way through. Then came the thud that seemed distant, lurching the *Sassanoa*'s bow down and her stern into the air. The wind caught the trimmed mainsail and pulled them sideways off the rock. When broadside to the wind and going over, Jacob finally unleashed the mainsail and let the boom fly. The wind spilled out; they were off the rock. His father leaned over the side of the boat to check for damage.

"No harm done," he said and grabbed the tiller. There had only been a thud, Jacob thought. His father steered them toward the channel. Jacob trimmed the jib, and they sped along with the wind and rocks behind them. The collision seemed never to have happened, and Jacob knew they would not talk about it— as if it were a secret they would have to keep from his dead grandfather.

Outside the harbor the wind blew twice as strong and the swells rose high into the air. The hull planed. Jacob sat on the rail and adjusted the jib sheet while his father sat on the transom so he could see over the bow. When they rose to the top of a swell, they could see out to sea as if from the top of a mountain. The bow sliced up one side of the wave and the stern coasted down the other side just as his great grandfather had designed her to do, and Jacob was immensely proud in that moment, thinking of his great grandfather's mind and hands creating such an efficient and worthy craft. More than that: the *Sassanoa* was a work of art, perfectly balanced between the wind and the ocean, that sat at her mooring in the morning as calmly as a sleeping dove.

Jacob looked back at his father, who grinned like a child, his open mouth and bright wide eyes pointed up at the blood-red sail as if the very idea of the wind moving a boat over water at such a speed was a discovery he had just made for the world.

As they coasted down a swell, Jacob leaned over and placed his hand on the side of the hull. He did not think of turning around even as they passed Damirscove Island. He could see in the windows of the old coast guard station there; at a certain height he could see in one window and out another. Europeans had settled on the treeless island, he knew, before Plymouth or Jamestown. They had fished there, and lived in cold shacks. Several hundred years later the coast guard had come, and now they were gone, too, and the island was empty except for the terns, gulls, herons, and snowy egrets that swarmed over the grass.

After Damirscove there were no other landmarks to gauge distance over water, and Jacob did not look back except to check his father's eyes darting from the sails to the ocean in perfect concentration. Jacob didn't care how far they sailed as long as his father continued to smile.

Jacob looked up at the sail and noticed how the pressure of the wind moved from one side to the other as his father shifted the lines and tiller. Some of the wind spilled out the side of the sail, swirled around back and caused a luff. With a slight adjustment they were back on track. Then Jacob noticed a frayed stay. Three or four of the metal threads that twisted around each other had snapped, which left two or three at the most to hold all the weight of the sail and the wind. Any number of bad things would happen, Jacob thought, if the rear stay broke. The mast would snap immediately, and might drag the boat over with this strong a wind. The weight of the keel would probably keep them upright. Even so, without the sail there was only the paddle. No motor. Jacob promised himself he would check all the rigging the next day.

"Dad, look." Jacob pointed up at the stay and as he pointed he knew he was also pointing a finger at his father for not keeping the boat up to his grandfather's standards. His father glanced up and saw the fray but did not seem concerned.

"It'll hold."

The wind did not vanish immediately, as often happened, but gradually, to Jacob's relief, until it was no longer necessary for his father to concentrate so hard on their heading. Jacob could tell his father's mind was on some other worry, probably to do with work.

"We should head in," Jacob said. He hadn't even looked back for some time. He wanted his father to be the first one.

His father did look and raised his eyebrows, not in shock but surprise, and so Jacob looked back, too. They were a good distance from shore. The wind usually switched in the evening, after a lull. This was that lull. They would just have to wait for the switch. With any luck it would be a south or west wind. In any case the water around the *Sassanoa* for as far as they could see in all directions was smooth and dull gray-green.

Jacob never noticed the cold when the sails were full, when there was action, but now, in the stillness, he rubbed the goose bumps on his arms.

His father pulled his sport coat collar up around his neck and looked down at the bilge. "Damn!" he yelled and yanked his briefcase off the floor. He brushed the water off the leather surface. "I don't think any water got inside." At first Jacob thought he was talking about the *Sassanoa*.

The sails were swaying now, like curtains, in the dim light. The horizon had just turned orange. It was not going to be a clear night; fog might even roll in from offshore. For the first time, Jacob noticed that his sneakers were soaked right through. That's why he was so cold. Under way, he seemed to lose all sensation, but now he could see that his feet rested in water that had hidden in the bilge while the boat was heeling. Their bow had dipped, riding the swells, but Jacob hadn't seen any water coming over.

His father let go of the tiller and the mainsheet. With no wind they couldn't control the *Sassanoa*'s direction. Jacob looked at the back of his father's hands, resting on top of the briefcase. With the dried sea salt on the tanned skin, Jacob thought his father looked like a man who had been out to sea a very long time, though the briefcase and suit jacket made it seem as if he was just on the way to the office. Jacob understood that the *Sassanoa* was leaking through the bilge, probably where the keel was bolted to the hull. When they thudded against the rock in New Wagon harbor, they must have loosened the joint.

"I think we're taking on," Jacob said.

"I know," his father said, not looking up. "I'm thinking."

Jacob was silent. He decided he had better think, too. As a matter of pride, his grandfather had never kept a motor on board. The hand-pump bailer was on the island, with the life jackets and flares, in the boat bag. His father went under the deck and rummaged around. He came out a moment later holding the anchor, a twenty-pound aluminum hook attached to a length of chain and rope. The water had risen two inches above the floorboards and was still rising. A lobster boat motored by on its way home a little ways to the west, but neither Jacob nor his father thought to wave.

His father held the paddle in one hand and the anchor in the other. Suddenly he stood up on the deck and waved the paddle in the direction of the lobster boat. "Hey! Hey!" They could see the man in yellow waders behind the wheel, looking forward, not back.

Jacob had never in his life seen his father or grandfather call for help while on the water. Jacob's heart pounded, and he was no longer cold or tired. He had been thinking about his mother's shepherd's pie, but now he saw what he should have seen before.

"What are we going to do?"

His father sat down. "We'll be fine. Let's see what the problem is down there." He lifted the hatch in the floorboards and stared down through the water to the bottom of the bilge. The compartment narrowed to the shape of a V, where Jacob could see the keel bolts protruding. His father removed his jacket, folded it carefully on top of his briefcase, and reached his hand down into the bilge.

"I can feel the water flowing in around one of the bolts. I think." He lifted his arm out. All the rollers had vanished now and the water was flat for as far as they could see. His father removed his shirt. Jacob was startled by the white skin and curly black hairs.

He recognized the future shape of his own body, but had trouble imagining himself covered with so much hair. His father ripped the shirt on a cleat, tore it into strips, and leaned back into the bilge. The water was so deep now that he had to crane his neck to keep his face from going underwater. He gave up trying and plunged both his arms and his head under the water. Jacob watched numbly as his father's back muscles bulged and strained against the skin. He popped out a moment later dripping and gulping for air.

"I wrapped the cloth around the bolt. Hand me the anchor and I'll pound it down. That should wedge the cloth in and stop the leak."

Jacob handed the anchor to his father, who went back down under water. Jacob heard the thud of the metal anchor smashing against the top of the bolt, and occasionally the sound of his father missing and hitting the wooden spine. His father came up for air and went back down. Finally he rested back, and set the anchor down. "That should do it."

Jacob nodded. His father was shivering violently. "Put on your jacket, dad."

"Yeah." After wrapping himself in the jacket for a moment and rubbing his arms, his father looked intently at his son. "We shouldn't have tried the trickiest bit."

"We'll fix it when we get back. We should probably replace those bolts anyway."

"You're right about that. Those bolts must be twenty-five years old. This is an old boat, you know. Let's get this water out of here. You start, will you? You'll have to use what's left of my shirt to sop it up, and then I'll start paddling."

Jacob picked up the shirt and soaked it in the water, but quickly realized his father was not thinking right. Instead of using the shirt, Jacob took off his shoe and started to scoop out the water. "The tide's going out," he said

"I know."

They were moving farther away from shore. His father paddled as Jacob scooped up water and dumped it over the side. His father kept looking down at his son, and Jacob guessed what he was thinking. He wanted to somehow hide it from his father, he didn't want his father to get angry with himself, but Jacob couldn't help it—the water was still rising.

His father sat down and stared back into the bilge. His feet were wet and he was shivering again. Jacob looked down, too, but in the darkness he couldn't see the bottom. His father removed his jacket again and thrust himself beneath the water. He stayed down so long Jacob almost touched the white skin of his father's back to make sure he was all right. Then his father burst out and stumbled back across the boat, landing against the tiller.

"Damn. It's not the bolt. There's a crack in one of the lower planks. One of the ribs must have pushed out when we hit and split the planks or something. I don't know. I can't patch it from inside."

His father's eyes widened when he saw his briefcase sitting on one of the seats. He lunged across the boat and fumbled with the latches.

"Let me," Jacob said, rising and standing next to his father, but his father pushed him away.

"I got it." The two latches clicked up and the briefcase popped open. His father grabbed the phone with his numb hands. He had to cradle it in one palm and aim with the index finger of the opposite hand at the POWER button. Jacob could see his father's teeth gleaming in the moonlight, but he turned his attention to the phone and waited for the yellow lights to appear on the panel. Nothing happened. His father pushed again, and again.

"The battery's dead. Didn't you turn the power off?" His father looked at the phone in total disbelief, and then at Jacob, who, to avoid looking at his father's eyes, also looked at the phone. He tried to remember if he had pushed the power button after talking to his mother. His father let out an awful noise, half growl, half scream, and threw the phone toward shore. Jacob heard it plop like a stone. His father picked up his briefcase, too, swung it against the deck of the boat with a crack, and then hurled that out as well. The white papers fluttered through the air like a flock of panicked terns before drifting slowly to the water and vanishing. The open briefcase tipped sideways and sank from view.

His father watched the place where it had been. Jacob watched his father and thought that they could have used the briefcase to bail. Maybe they could stay ahead of the leak until morning, when someone would see them for sure. "Maybe someone will see us out here tonight."

His father looked up at the rigging, his shoulder blades pinching together. "Not with red canvas. We'll have to patch the crack from the outside. Hand me my shirt there and the anchor."

Jacob rested them on the deck as his father removed his shoes and slacks, and he groaned when his body slid into the cold water. His white arm came up and grasped the shirt and anchor. He put the anchor back on the deck.

"You'll have to dangle the anchor over the side for me while I use the edge of it to stuff the rag into the crack." His father's voice was already shaky, and his teeth chattered.

Jacob leaned over the side and watched his father vanish into the dark water.

"Give me a little more slack," his father said after coming up for air. Then he went back down again, and Jacob heard faint taps on the hull. His father came back up for air. "It's a long narrow crack," he said. "It must bend inward but we can't get to it from the inside without ripping up the floor. Even then I think it's out of reach from the inside."

Jacob didn't want to say anything. He wasn't sure of the situation. His father went down again, tapped, and came up. This time he let out a long moan before sucking in air and going back down. Tapping turned to banging. Jacob could see the outline of the silver anchor swinging through the water below. His father was swinging as hard as he could through the water at the crack. Jacob had an idea which plank it was. The last thud was muffled. He looked down to see his father pulling back on the anchor.

"No!" Jacob said, but it was too late. His father jimmied the anchor out and then came up for air. Jacob pulled the anchor aboard and reached his own arm down into the bilge. He could not reach the plank his father had been hitting, but now he could feel the flow of water rushing in where the anchor had made a gash.

"I'm too cold," his father said.

Jacob turned and wrapped his hands around one of his father's arms and pulled. His father kicked and lunged up, eventually getting his stomach over the gunwale and grabbing the edge of the seat. Jacob put his hands and arm around his father's waist, feeling the hair on his father's back press against his face, and tugged. The flesh was cold to his lips and hands, but Jacob was afraid to let go, even when his father was safely on the seat.

His father pulled away, rose to his feet, and found the anchor. He dropped it, and then clamped it between his hands and swung it over his head like an axe. The anchor bounced off the deck and fell to the floor. His father reached into the water and lifted it over his head again.

"No, no!" Jacob reached for his father, who was using the last of his full strength to swing the anchor against the deck. This time the anchor bounced into the ocean. They both watched as the chain and fifty feet of rope snaked out of the boat, snapped into the air, and disappeared. Jacob felt embarrassed for having cried out.

His father sat down on the seat. The water rose almost to his knee. Jacob shook, but his father was beyond that stage. His eyes drooped.

"We'll have to swim." His father barely mumbled, he was so groggy with cold.

Jacob nodded. The tide had taken them further out. Jacob realized they might have been able to swim it pretty easily if they had started out when they first noticed the leak. Now it was farther away and his father was tired. Even in late August the water was frigid, and they wouldn't have much time before hypothermia set in. Jacob was an excellent swimmer. He swam for a team at school, but that was in warm water at an indoor pool. A long string of lights followed the shoreline of New Wagon harbor and seemed close enough to touch.

"You swim for shore and get help."

Jacob couldn't see his father's lips moving. "No."

"Don't argue. Take the paddle and swim as well as you can. Don't let go. Go now."

Jacob stood on the gunwale with the paddle in his hand looking down into the water. The deck was less than a foot off the surface. He eased himself in with the paddle gripped in his hand.

"I'll be right back," Jacob yelled, but there was no response. He could see the silhouette of his father's head and thought about checking on him, but decided he had better keep going, focusing on the brightest light on shore, probably someone's dock, and kicking with all the force he could muster. He felt strong at first, but then grew stiff, his legs moving in slow motion. He looked behind him. The outline of the sails seemed lower in the water. He turned and kicked harder, afraid to lose sight of the dock but also thinking maybe the wind would still come up. Soon he could barely move his legs, and the water felt warmer as he turned onto his back to rest. His thoughts slowed. Tomorrow, he thought, they would tow the *Sassanoa* to the island and patch the hole. He wanted to call out to his father and tell him about the plan, but before he could, the dark triangle set against the stars sank into the blue-black horizon, and there was no sign of the pale shoulders and arms of the man who had promised him all those summer afternoons when he would finally sail alone.